Paws for Love

Love Unleashed

Sit, Stay, Love

Fetching Sweetness

Paws for Love

Paws for Love

DANA MENTINK

HARVEST HOUSE PUBLISHERS
EUGENE, OREGON

Cover by Left Coast Design

Cover Photo © Eric Isselee / Shutterstock

The author is represented by MacGregor Literary, Inc.

This is a work of fiction. Names, characters, places, and incidents are products of the author's imagination or are used fictitiously. Any resemblance to actual persons, living or dead, is entirely coincidental.

PAWS FOR LOVE

Copyright © 2017 by Dana Mentink
Published by Harvest House Publishers
Eugene, Oregon 97402
www.harvesthousepublishers.com

ISBN 978-0-7369-6625-2 (pbk.)
ISBN 978-0-7369-6626-9 (eBook)

Library of Congress Cataloging-in-Publication Data

Names: Mentink, Dana, author.
Title: Paws for love / Dana Mentink.
Description: Eugene, Oregon : Harvest House Publishers, [2017]
Identifiers: LCCN 2016034916 (print) | LCCN 2016040943 (ebook) | ISBN 9780736966252 (paperback) | ISBN 9780736966269 (e-book)
Subjects: | BISAC: FICTION / Christian / Romance. | GSAFD: Christian fiction. | Love stories.
Classification: LCC PS3613.E496 P39 2017 (print) | LCC PS3613.E496 (ebook) | DDC 813/.6—dc23
LC record available at https://lccn.loc.gov/2016034916

Printed in the United States of America

16 17 18 19 20 21 22 23 24 / BP-SK / 10 9 8 7 6 5 4 3 2 1

*To the selfless volunteers at the Animal
Rescue Foundation who gave us Junie,
ten pounds of joy and mischief in a fur coat.*

*Let your light shine before others,
that they may see your good deeds
and glorify your Father in heaven.*

MATTHEW 5:16

One

Misty Agnelli crouched behind the Sherman tank, ignoring the detonations and nervously chewing a stick of Juicy Fruit that had lost its flavor hours earlier. Through puffs of smoke, Dirk staggered into view, face bloody, rifle at the ready, and a pack slung over his shoulder.

He coughed, swiped at the wound on his face, sank to one knee, lowered the rifle, and yanked the pack off his shoulder. She was close enough to make out the beads of sweat on his grimy forehead. Digging through the backpack, he found the precious violin and yanked it free. The action set her teeth on edge.

Easy, she silently commanded. He should be gentler with the delicate neck of the instrument. But what did she know about battle behavior? Maybe the bombs were getting to him.

Dirk plucked once, very softly. *A perfect pizzicato*, she thought with satisfaction. The action loosed one note into the war-torn air. A lump formed in her throat at the sound of that note, which vibrated with heartache and the horror of battle, a longing for home, a loss of innocence, an affirmation of humanity. It was lovely, if slightly flat, that one tragic note. Before the sound died away, Dirk sank to the ground with one last bark.

Bark?

The spell broken, Misty blinked in surprise from her hiding place. A dog streaked by, yowling furiously. The little creature zinged in three excited circles so fast it was no more than a blur of pointy ears and whirling tail. From somewhere behind Misty, a notepad was hurled to the ground, followed by a stream of language. Yelling—the antithesis of music.

"Cut!" Mr. Wilson hollered in a voice so loud that Misty ducked reflexively, fearing something might be thrown in her direction. "Did that really just happen?" he thundered, ripping off his baseball cap and slapping it against his thigh. "Tell me that did not just happen during our last run-through before we roll film. Can somebody enlighten me? Was I lost in la-la land for a minute?"

Misty was not sure if he was speaking to her or his director's assistant. Best to remain silent.

Dirk, known to his legion of adoring fans as Lawrence Tucker, rose to his feet. They'd done an amazing job on his makeup, and somehow he appeared much younger than his sixty-three years, every inch the exhausted American GI. He shoved the violin back in the pack and held it out, as if waiting for someone to relieve him of it.

No one appeared to be stepping forward. He looked as though he might toss it aside. The violin was not a Stradivarius, to be sure, but she could not stand the thought of it hitting the ground, so in spite of her jumping nerves, she hastened closer and took it. Might as well retune while she had the chance. No one would notice her, she hoped.

As she grabbed for the violin, Lawrence gave her a distracted nod. He cleared his throat. "You can't blame this small creature. We're soldiers. To quote Charles Spurgeon, 'The Lord gets his best soldiers out of the highlands of affliction.'"

Was he giving a speech or making casual conversation? She couldn't tell. Even in their initial lessons, he'd baffled her. Then again, people's behavior often baffled Misty.

"What soldier wouldn't exhibit such behavior?" Another question that fortunately did not seem to require an answer. Lawrence began to call for the dog with no result.

Misty could practically hear Mr. Wilson's teeth grinding.

"It's a dog, not a soldier," he snapped. "This is a film. We make believe here. There is no war, remember?" Misty heard him mutter something about actors under his breath.

Lawrence blinked and offered a wan smile. "It's all so real to me. Sometimes I forget."

"I don't," Mr. Wilson snapped, "not when we pay through the nose for each delay. Your dog is a menace. It snapped at the makeup artist, chewed the gaffer's plans, and I'm pretty sure he peed on my boots while I was napping." He pointed to the expensive leather footwear. "There's an aroma."

"In wartime…" Lawrence began a mournful diatribe. Then he caught the director's exasperated expression and gave himself a shake. "Sorry. Movie set. I got it. Jellybean will settle into his role, I'm sure."

"He doesn't have a role. He's a dog." Wilson sighed. "I'm sorry, but you're going to have to send it off the set. Hire a sitter, put him in a kennel, something."

Lawrence looked as though he had just been bayoneted. Misty's grandmother would be reeling. Nana Bett adored the actor, watching all of his movies often enough to have the lines memorized. She'd thrown her cane aside and literally danced a jig when the movie people had contacted Misty to tutor him in basic violin. Then she'd set about using all her considerable powers of persuasion to convince Misty to take the gig. It had not been an easy task. Nana Bett would be horrified to hear the star was about to have his dog evicted from the set.

"You will be working with the greatest actor ever to grace the silver screen," Nana had breathed.

The greatest actor ever to grace the silver screen straightened and beamed a look at the director as if he were a vile German commandant. "Jellybean must stay."

Mr. Wilson straightened to his full five feet three. It didn't help, as Lawrence was a good six inches taller. "No animals on set. He can't stay, Lawrence."

"Then," Lawrence said after a slow exhale, "we are at an impasse, Director Wilson. I cannot continue. I must depart."

Wilson gaped. "Are you saying you'll walk off the set if your mutt isn't allowed to stay?"

Lawrence glared. "I would communicate it much more eloquently, but yes."

Wilson's cheeks flushed scarlet. "You're under contract, Mr. Tucker."

He lifted a lazy shoulder. "So sue me."

Mr. Wilson threw his baseball cap on the floor. The dog zipped in and snatched it up.

"Gimme that," Wilson snapped, but he had no hope of catching Jellybean as he darted around the director's boots. "You see? This is intolerable. That's my lucky hat, and now it has tooth holes in it."

"Well, it's a disgraceful excuse for a hat," Lawrence said. "Who wears a hat advertising mayonnaise anyway?"

The tension between the two men built to a crescendo, so Misty did what she always did when her stomach clenched and the world closed in. She stepped away, took out the violin, shrank back into herself, and played pianissimo, soft enough not to attract attention. She stroked the bow gently over the strings, a sonata, quiet as a whisper. Her pulse slowed to keep time. Eyes closed, she mentally calculated the degree to which the A string needed to be tuned.

Pressure on her shoes caused her eyes to fly open. The little set crasher known as Jellybean sat on her feet, staring up, small blackish-brownish body quivering, little pointy terrier ears alert. He resembled Toto from the *Wizard of Oz*, she thought, though she could not imagine this specimen getting stuffed into a bicycle basket.

Lawrence looked awestruck. "Please play a little more, Ms. Agnelli. Jellybean is enthralled."

Misty looked at all the faces staring at her—Mr. Wilson, Lawrence Tucker, the script manager, and the man just walking in with a tray of coffee—and her cheeks went hot. Then cold. Prickles teased her skin. "I don't, er…"

She lowered the violin, and the dog leapt upward. She barely caught him with one arm as she clutched the violin in the other. Jellybean swiped a pink tongue under her chin, panting hot breath onto her neck.

"It likes you," the director said in wonderment. "I didn't think it liked anyone."

"I…uh…" Misty held the dog as if it were a live grenade. She wanted desperately to put the thing down and let it run away along with all the attention that was focused on her at that very moment. A sick feeling flashed through her, the one that meant, *Run, Misty, escape at all costs!*

Wilson and Lawrence exchanged a loaded glance. "Are you thinking what I'm thinking?" Wilson said.

"I am indeed." Lawrence beamed. "Ms. Agnelli can both tutor me on the violin and be a companion to Jellybean."

Her jaw dropped. "Me?"

"Great." Wilson retrieved the hat Jellybean had discarded before he'd leapt into Misty's arms. "You're Tucker's new assistant until this film wraps," the director said, turning toward his camera guy.

"But I'm the music tutor—"

"Yeah, you'll do that too."

Her mind reeled. "I'm not a movie person."

"Uh-huh." Wilson checked something off on a clipboard.

"I'm not actually a people person either." Never had been. Never would be.

He did not look up. "You're not here for people. Just Tucker and the dog." He considered his words. "No offense, Mr. Tucker."

Misty's mind could not grasp it. The dog wriggled, nosing at the violin strings. "But I *can't*."

Wilson finally looked at her through his reading glasses. "Why not?"

Why not? Because all these people are staring at me. Because I want to go back to my apartment and play my violin. Because I am a thirty-four-year-old woman with a disastrous case of social anxiety who would rather crawl over barbed wire than interact with this gaggle of people. Thank goodness that last bit hadn't slipped past her terrified lips.

"I've got to go home," she managed.

"Don't sweat it. We'll pay you extra for your added duties. You teach lessons via Skype, right? So you can still carry on with your music job from here. We'll set you up in a trailer. Brenda, work that out, huh?" he called to an assistant who could not be much older than some of Misty's high school violin pupils.

"But…"

The director walked away, leaving Misty, the dog, and a violin with an out-of-tune A string.

Lawrence patted her on the shoulder, ignoring the menacing growl from Jellybean. "You know what they say about those 'highlands of affliction.'"

With the wriggling dog and the violin in her grasp, and a dozen movie people circling around her, Misty was beginning to feel very afflicted indeed. The feeling intensified when Jellybean gave her a final slurp, catapulted from her arms, and beelined toward town.

∽

Bill Woodson managed to get his six-foot frame sprawled next to Fiona and the little dollhouse he'd built her in the front of his Chocolate Heaven Candy Shop. She solemnly handed him the boy doll. His heart skipped a beat as he looked into the soon-to-be four-year-old's clear azure eyes, so blue, so innocent.

He considered the tiny wooden doll in his big fingers. "Should I, er, put him upstairs in the playroom?"

She nodded.

He put the doll in the specified place. Now what? What was the proper doll scenario to act out with a little girl? Sweat broke out on his forehead. "Maybe he could, you know, do some sit-ups or push-ups. How about that?"

He saw from the crimp in her lip that he'd disappointed her. Again. "No? What about cooking? He could go make some chocolates in the kitchen or fix the car." He held up the toy car. "I think it's due for an oil change."

She shook her head, sending the blond curls bouncing.

He scrunched down lower so he could look her in the eyes. "Fee, I'm sorry I don't know how to play dolls. If you could tell me what to do, I'd try. Okay?"

Instead, she sat down in the child-sized chair he'd set there for a makeshift play corner and picked up the same tattered storybook. Sticking her two middle fingers in her mouth, she sent him another one of those looks as she held out the book.

What was it about that ragged old thing that made her return to it practically every day in the last three months since he'd taken custody of her? "Fee," he started, his gaze fastening on a children's CD player, "how about we have a sing-along again?" He clicked on the music, prepared to do a full-on solo rendition of "The Farmer in the Dell." The music started up, and he was pleased to see that Fiona had begun to clap her hands. *Yes, Uncle Bill for the win!*

An unexpected noise made them both jump. He thought at first that a bird had struck the window, so he opened the door to see. A dog shot through his legs and raced around the shop in dizzying circles. It was the color of dark chocolate in some places and caramel in others, about the size of a loaf of bread. Fiona clutched the book to her chest.

"It's okay," he called. "I'll get it. It won't hurt you."

The nutty terrier-type critter darted around, sniffing the air and avoiding Bill's grasping hands. He lunged and regrouped, but the thing was fast. "Come here, dog," he commanded.

Finally, it trotted over to Fiona and sat quite suddenly at her feet, staring at her with unblinking black eyes.

Bill froze.

Fiona stared and crouched to get a better look.

The dog wagged his curl of a tail and rasped a tongue across her cheek.

She clapped her small hand to the wet spot, and he was afraid she was going to cry. He took a step in her direction, stunned when she dropped down on the floor by the dog, who promptly rolled over, stubby legs bicycling in the air.

Fiona looked to him.

"Dogs do that when they want you to scratch their tummies. Let me do it. We don't know if he's friendly or not."

Bill eased closer, ready to snatch for the dog's collar, when a woman jogged through the door. She stepped on the discarded boy doll and slipped, landing on her bottom on the laminate wood floor he'd recently installed.

"Are you hurt?" he said, springing to offer assistance.

"No." Reluctantly, she took his hand and climbed to her feet.

She was tall for a woman, with long, straight, golden-brown hair and brown eyes. She had a strong nose, full lips, and a slight dimple in her chin. Her complexion was hard to figure as she now blushed a fiery pink.

She picked up the boy doll, whose head had snapped off. "Sorry. I, uh, decapitated him."

"No problem. I'll make another."

She handed it over. Her fingers were calloused but long and delicate, the nails square and blunt. He wondered what she did for a living.

"Is this your dog?" he said, pointing to the animal, who was now enjoying a tentative belly scratch from Fiona. The dog wriggled helpfully to put his belly in better alignment with the little fingers.

"No."

He considered. "So you were just running in here at this moment...to buy chocolate?"

She toyed with the zipper on her windbreaker. "Uh, no, I was actually after the dog, but he's not mine. I mean, I'm the tutor." She shook her head. "Not the dog's tutor. I Tucker Mr. Tutor. I mean, I tutor Mr. Tucker."

He grasped the straw. "Ah. Wait a minute. You're with the film crew, aren't you? I think I saw you when I delivered the chocolate fondue yesterday. I'm Bill Woodson."

Her face took on a dreamy look. "Luscious." She started. "Oh, um, I meant the fondue. It was great. Everyone loved it."

He laughed. "Thank you. My special recipe. So you're not an actor? Do you work for the director, then?"

Her brows puckered. "I'm not completely sure." There was something in her face, a painful confusion that made him want to help. With what? He didn't even know what they were talking about, and even now she was shifting on her feet as if she wanted to grab the dog and run for the exit.

His cell phone rang. After looking at the screen, he said, "Sorry, I have to take this. I'll just be a minute, and then maybe I can get you a cup of coffee."

She began to protest, but he held up his hand and stepped away to take the call, which turned out to be an order from Vivian Buckley for three dozen chocolate cream balls and assorted caramels for the Lady Bird Hotel. He mentally high-fived himself. Orders were slowly picking up, thanks to the film crew rolling into the tiny town of Albatross, California. Maybe he'd have enough extra this month to get Fiona a bike, at least an old one that he could fix up.

"Sorry," he said. "I'm…" But he turned to find that both the dog and the blushing woman were gone.

Fiona's head was quirked a bit to one side, as if she was realizing the same thing he was.

He hadn't even gotten the woman's name.

Two

Lawrence sat rigidly on a chair in Misty's newly assigned trailer the next morning, mouth pinched in concentration, the violin resting on his left collarbone. The window was partially open, letting in a whiff of the ocean.

Misty gave him an encouraging nod. "That's great, Mr. Tucker. Now let's try the G major scale again, okay?"

Jellybean sat licking his paws. When Lawrence raked the bow over the strings, Jellybean let out a tortured whimper, scurried across the worn linoleum, and leapt on top of the bed. It was only through effort that Misty did not do the same.

Lawrence smiled indulgently. "He's sensitive. Loud noises awaken tragic memories in his heart. I rescued him, you know."

She repositioned Lawrence's fingers on the bow. "From where?"

"A frozen lake."

It was not the answer she'd been expecting. Jellybean, she'd guessed, might have belonged to an indulgent elderly dowager who fed him cake and named him as sole beneficiary in her will.

"It was in Minnesota six years ago." His eyes glazed over as he recounted the memory. "I was on a break from a film shoot. I took a walk in the woods. I'm a method actor, you see, and I was playing the part of a man hiking through the wilderness to save his daughter who had been kidnapped by a motorcycle gang." His eyes glittered. "That was an amazing film. You could feel the cold, the isolation, the man-versus-nature theme. Critics went wild for it."

Misty made a mental note to ask her grandmother if she'd seen that one. "And you found Jellybean?" she encouraged. Lawrence had a way of drifting off the conversational path, she'd learned in their short acquaintance.

"It was freezing, and as I turned to go back, I saw this fuzzy head poking out from a hole in the ice. He was whimpering and shivering, so weak, tiny paws about to lose their hold. The ice was thin, but I could not leave this helpless animal there to slip under the frigid waters."

"So you went out on the lake to get him?" Misty looked from Lawrence to Jellybean, who was making a nest of her blankets.

"Step-by-step, inch-by-inch. It was a close call."

Lawrence let loose with another squeaking attempt at the G scale. Jellybean whined. Misty whined internally.

"Less pressure on the strings. Retract the weight of your bowing arm back into your shoulder."

Lawrence tried again, and this time he produced a fairly decent sound. He sat back, beaming. "Thank you, Misty. I may call you Misty, mayn't I?"

"Sure. All my students do."

"And you may call me Lawrence. We are going to be lifelong friends," he said, flourishing the bow around like a conductor's baton. She made a subtle grab for it before he could break off the fragile tip by knocking it against the cupboard. Lifelong friends. She didn't have many of those, for sure. This eccentric man was not what she imagined a close friend would look like, but how was she to know?

"Now you." He sat back in the chair.

"Me? What me?"

"You must play for me. You will be my muse."

She let out a relieved sigh. "Oh, I'm not muse material."

"Play for me, my girl. Let me disappear into the music. It's the only thing that I will remember when I am fallen on the field of battle." He slouched back in the chair and closed his eyes.

Misty looked from Lawrence to the ball of blanket-wrapped dog on the bed. Outside, a bustle of activity indicated the crew was emerging to begin the Thursday preparations. "Um, okay. What shall I play?"

He didn't answer, so she launched into a stretch of Paganini. The music filled up the corners of the trailer. She continued on, the caprice dancing and twirling through the small space.

The swaddled lump rose from the bed and ran to her, once again sitting on her feet, nose quivering, looking much as he must have appeared to Lawrence as he climbed out of the water onto the ice of the frozen pond. She was not sure what emotion was coursing through that canine heart. Was he happy? Troubled? Ready to pee on her sneakers?

She stopped.

Jellybean barked.

Lawrence sighed. "Incredible how I can disappear into my music."

His music? Maybe he was attempting to be funny. So far he'd only managed to produce a painful G major scale. Of course the actual movie music would be dubbed in, but at least he would know violin mechanics well enough to be convincing on-screen. One more lesson maybe, he'd be prepped, and she could go home. Any follow-up could be done by Skype with a computer screen. The thought bolstered her.

"Mr. Tucker…" She caught his disapproving glance. "Lawrence, I don't think I can stay here for your shoot after today. You've learned enough of the violin basics, and I'm sure you can get another dog sitter."

He blinked and looked closely at her as if seeing her for the first time. "Most people would do anything to work with a star on a movie set."

She sighed. "I'm not most people."

"That is true." He pursed his lips, head cocked slightly to one side. "You're scared, aren't you?"

"What?"

"Scared." He waved a hand toward the outside. "Of all this."

"No, I'm…" Her words died away.

How did he know? She had not thought him capable of noticing what she tried diligently to hide. Scared of crowds, closed spaces, scared of people, of life.

"That's the thing about being an actor," he said. "I can read people, study them, extract their motivations for my own purposes. It's clinical in a way. I don't engage in other people's emotions, but I can recognize and use them as one would use a tool. I see fear in you, Misty Agnelli." He pointed a finger at her. "You are a woman in hiding."

Her palms felt sweaty against the wood of the violin. She held it tighter for comfort. "I need to go home."

He examined every detail of her face as if he was absorbing it for a later purpose. *Creepy*, Misty thought to herself.

Absently, he reached down to caress Jellybean, recoiling when the dog growled at him.

The silent staring stretched on, and she wriggled like a bug specimen skewered on a pin. How could she politely get away from this strange man? Was he waiting for her to say something? She racked her brain, trying to think of something appropriate. To her great surprise, he started to hum.

"Took me a minute to remember the tune. Can you play this one?"

She listened to him hum a song she had not heard in a very long time.

"Something about 'this little light of mine,'" Lawrence sang in a fairly decent tenor. "You know it, Misty?"

She did. She'd sung it in Sunday school and heard it belted out in churches in which she'd never felt at home but had lingered on the fringes, quiet and invisible. Mechanically, she played the melody on her violin, eliciting vigorous tail wagging from Jellybean.

"Splendid." Lawrence got up and went to the door. "I've got a meet and greet with the people of Albatross today at ten at the Lady Bird Hotel. Jellybean should come. Celebrity dogs always get a good reaction from crowds."

"Mr. Tucker, er, Lawrence, didn't you hear what I said? I can't stay here. You need to find another dog sitter."

He continued to hum. "Misty Agnelli," he proclaimed as he threw open the trailer door, "it's time to let it shine!"

What was he talking about?

"Lawrence," she tried again. "Do you need to sit down?"

"Let's go, Jellybean," he called.

With a swish, Jellybean dove back under the rumpled covers. Misty wished with all her strength that she could do the same.

Bill led Fiona into the preschool classroom where Dina Everly was putting Play-Doh onto colorful trays. Her hair was pulled back into a blond ponytail, and he wondered why twenty-five-year-olds looked so darn young compared to his thirty-six. Of course, since the accident three months before that had taken his brother and sister-in-law, he'd probably aged a good decade or two. Now he understood why his own parents sometimes had that haggard look when he was growing up. Parenting was not a game for the timid.

Dina knelt down to talk to Fiona, who cowered behind his leg, clutching his knee. "Hey, Fiona. Glad to see you."

Fiona clung tighter.

Ms. Everly had told him quick goodbyes were best.

"Yeah, uh, you have a great morning. I'll be back at one to get you, okay?"

Fiona sniffed. *Oh dear, sweet Lord*, he prayed. *Please don't let her cry.* His insides felt as if they were being seared by a red-hot poker when he had to leave her crying.

Ms. Everly snatched up a toy teddy bear that was nearly Fiona's size. "Here's Honey Bear. Take her to the reading corner, Fiona. I just put out a new book there for you. It's about frogs. I know how you like to read about frogs." She gestured to a girl with pigtails wearing two macaroni necklaces. "Macy, can you go show Fiona our new frog book?"

The girl waved to Fiona, who trailed after her to the reading corner, Honey Bear in tow. Fiona's mouth was pinched, but she wasn't crying. Miss Dina was good. He heaved a sigh and followed the teacher to the door. She offered him a manila envelope and extended a palm.

In exchange, he fished the papers from his back pocket and handed them over.

"I'll take a look," she said. "See you later."

He eased out the door and stopped on the porch, eyeing the worn Happy Days Preschool sign. "This the next project?"

She nodded. "The paint's peeling and one of the hooks is about to let loose. Can you fix it?"

"'Course I can."

She grinned. "Is there anything you can't do?"

He felt the familiar twinge of shame. "Think you already know the answer to that." Resisting the urge to look in again on Fiona, he hurried back to the shop and stowed the envelope on a shelf. The smell of chocolate greeted him, and his memory took him right back to his mother Ada's kitchen. Her candy-making sessions were the best days of his life, his success measured in easy moments with her and the simple bliss of those pans full of homemade candies. He surveyed the conching machine and the enormous mixer.

Was he really doing this? Was he really running a chocolate shop in the tiny town of Albatross? Three months ago he would not have thought twice about starting such a risky new venture. Three months ago he never would have dreamed that he would abruptly become a parent to his preschool-aged niece. He swallowed down an unaccustomed feeling that he took to be fear.

Gunther waved a freckled hand from behind the counter. "Finished boxing the bonbons."

Bill was pleased to see that his new hire, seventy-year-old Gunther, was wearing the neat white apron Bill had insisted on and the paper hat that covered his perfectly bald head. Bill donned his own apron and hat, took his place next to Gunther, and loaded up the peanut butter puffs and chocolate-dipped strawberries he'd prepared starting at three a.m. in the shop while Fiona slept soundly upstairs across the hallway from his own tiny bedroom.

Gunther pushed his glasses up on his face and moved to the chalkboard easel. "What you want it to say?"

"Just list what we've got in the shop today, and write something about the grand opening tomorrow."

Gunther raised an eyebrow. "How grand's it gonna be?"

"I'm getting balloons. That's pretty grand, isn't it?"

He raised the other eyebrow.

"You just wait, Gunther. This is going to be plenty impressive. A tour bus is coming to check out the film site. One hundred candy-loving tourists, and they're all going to want chocolate."

"What if they don't like chocolate?"

Bill laughed. "Gonna have to work on your optimism, friend."

Gunther snorted. "I'm a senior citizen working for minimum wage in a candy shop. Where's the rosy side of that?"

"You could be the laundryman working for a diaper service company."

Gunther let loose with a cackle. "All right," he said, waving a stick of neon-colored chalk at Bill. "I'll make the sign. You go spread your joy around with those movie nuts."

"Nothin' better than chocolate with nuts," Bill said as he gathered the candy-filled boxes and headed out.

The Lady Bird seemed like a particularly grand name to Bill when he'd first heard it. It was a two-story Victorian structure that could use a good repainting. The tall windows along the front of the building were framed by fancy wood trellises, and a porch sported cozy cushioned rocking chairs. He'd learned from Gunther that the place was actually more of a bed-and-breakfast with five guest rooms and a paneled sitting room with a slate-faced fireplace. He was happy to see the fireplace was not in service now as he let himself in and set down the boxes on the table provided. The place was done in soothing blues and sea foam greens that gave off a beach vibe. There were entirely too many knickknacks for his taste—jars of shells, pelican table lamps, and fussy photo frames with mermaids painted on the glass.

The owner, Vivian Buckley, a slender woman with a long, graying braid down her back, was already busily working the room, chatting with the dozen Albatross residents and tourists who had staked out the best chairs waiting for their meet and greet with Lawrence Tucker.

As Bill finished fanning out the napkins in what he figured was a pleasing arrangement and loaded the chocolates onto silver trays, he heard a yip from underneath the table. It was a terrier much like the one that had busted into his shop, only this one was the color of hazelnut ganache and chubbier around the middle. It was curled up on a pet bed, and he had bumped the cushion with his boot. "Sorry, dog-o."

"Tinka," Vivian said, looking up. "Come here, baby."

Tinka pattered over to Vivian and, with one impressive leap, jumped into her arms.

The front doors opened, and the star of the film trundled in. Up close, Lawrence looked much older than he did in the one movie that Bill had seen. He was shorter too. His graying hair was cut close, brows darker than his hair, eyes quick as a squirrel's as he immediately shook the hand of the nearest lady who goggled at him.

He moved on to the next and the next, but Bill's attention was drawn to the woman in the back, the one who had chased the dog she was now holding into his shop.

She looked, in a word, terrified. Back pressed to the cluttered sideboard, she held the dog under her chin as if to shield herself. *From what?* he wondered. The small group of Lawrence Tucker's adoring fans who had arrived ahead of the pack? No worries there, he thought as he squeezed over to her. The fans had eyes for no one but the star.

"Hey there," he said. "You in charge of this critter again?"

She blinked and nodded. "I told Lawrence I'm leaving, but I just sort of get swept along, like he's a planet with his own gravity field or something."

Bill chuckled. "I know people like that. Is this his dog?"

"Yes. Jellybean."

"Is he friendly?" Bill asked, putting out a hand.

"No."

Bill took his hand away. Her eyes continued to slide toward the door with longing in their brown depths, and she swayed gently from foot to foot. "Don't like crowds?" he guessed.

She started. "Is it that obvious? I was trying to blend." She shivered. "Too many people in here. Not enough oxygen."

Claustrophobic? He offered his warmest smile. "I'm Bill Woodson. Never got your name."

"Misty," she said quietly, hoisting the dog a little higher. "Misty Agnelli. I am...I *was* Mr. Tucker's violin tutor, but I'm leaving," she repeated firmly.

"So you mentioned. Why?"

"He doesn't need me."

They both looked at Tucker, who had the entire room riveted.

"I grew up not far from Albatross, you know," he told the group. "Went to high school right up the coast."

Vivian Buckley beamed a smile that was a little too bright to be sincere. "It's true," she said. "And you even had a local girl for a sweetheart too."

Tucker gazed at her, his smile never wavering. "Ah, Viv. I was just getting to that."

"I'm sure you were." She glared at him as she settled into an upholstered chair, stroking her dog's silky ears.

Bill perked up. This was an interesting turn of events.

"Yes, your very own Vivian Buckley—" Tucker was interrupted by Jellybean, who let out a shrill bark. All heads swiveled toward Misty. Her face flushed a cherry-cream red.

She let out a groan as Lawrence began to wax eloquent about his dog. The stares were fastened on Misty and Jellybean now.

"Can I make it to the door?" she whispered.

"I think you're caught," Bill whispered back.

"Oh yes, let me take a moment to introduce you to my faithful companion, Jellybean. Ms. Agnelli, bring him over, won't you? This is Misty Agnelli. She's a violin virtuoso who is helping me brush up on my skills. She teaches lessons on Skype, in case any of you have a budding violinist at home."

Misty stood frozen as the group stared in fascination. Bill reached out a hand and put it on her rigid shoulder.

"Come on," he whispered, "I'll walk with you."

He braced an arm around her and propelled her forward. They reached Lawrence, who took the now growling Jellybean.

Misty immediately backed up, pressing into Bill. Slowly, he rested a hand on her shoulder and gave a gentle squeeze, guiding her back to the fringes of the room where she seemed most comfortable.

"There's an interesting story about how this dog came into my life," Lawrence began.

Bill noticed an elaborate eye roll from Vivian. What was going on with these two? As Lawrence droned on, Jellybean caught sight of Tinka, curled on Vivian's lap.

Jellybean stiffened, barked, and wriggled so violently that Tucker lowered him to the floor. The dog shot toward Tinka. The startled female took off. In a moment, both dogs were doing laps around the room, knocking over the ornate frames and upsetting a jar of shells that crashed to the floor and broke. Then when a late-arriving guest pushed open the door, Tinka streaked through the gap, followed by Jellybean.

"Stop them!" Vivian shrieked.

Misty did not waste a moment. She sprinted out of the hotel like a racehorse headed for the finish line.

Albatross was turning out to be a pretty interesting town, Bill thought, as he followed on Misty's heels.

Three

Bill emerged on the street in time to see Misty vanishing around the corner. He took off in pursuit and, by way of his long legs, caught up in half a block.

"You're fast for a violin player."

She shot him a glance. Amusement? Annoyance? Something in between?

He'd gone for charming and landed somewhere short of the mark. It unsettled him. The Woodson charm was foolproof. He'd always had it, even when the rest of his attributes added up to a big, fat zero. But this was a new town, new people. Maybe his charm wouldn't get him very far here. His gut tightened as he considered how folks would treat him if they knew.

Don't go there, Bill.

"I see him." She pointed to a path etched into the grassy bank beside the road.

A black rump was just vanishing down the slope.

"He's headed to the beach," Bill said. "Typical tourist."

Keeping a few paces ahead of him, Misty seemed immune to

his humor as she ran across the street and started down the trail. It was steep and rocky in some places where a recent winter storm had eroded the path. They slipped and slid their way downward. When he reached for her hand at a difficult spot, her brown eyes widened.

"I'm okay," she said, a moment before she lost her footing and landed on her palms in the grit. She sighed as he helped her up. "I'm not making a very good impression, am I? This is the second time I've fallen down in your presence."

He laughed. "I wish I could say women fall for me all the time, but my mother used to wash my mouth out with a bar of green soap when I lied. I can still taste it. Wretched stuff."

After a long moment, a wry smile twisted her mouth and transformed her like the sun peeping through the clouds. "Well, thanks." The shuttered look returned. "Really, though. I can look for Jellybean and...the other dog."

"Tinka. She belongs to Vivian, the hotel owner."

"I'll find them. I don't want to take you away from your work."

He glanced at his watch. "It's only eleven. I don't have to pick up Fiona at preschool until one. I have a couple of hours to spare for dog searching. Besides, all these tourists coming into town are a boon to my business, and I think folks are as interested in Jellybean as they are in the actors." Truth was, he should be back at the shop, prepping for that tour bus full of movie buffs that would arrive the next day. But he'd never turned down someone who needed help, even if they didn't know they needed it.

Misty continued on without comment. She was only a chin shorter than him and looked strong, though not athletic. The wind grabbed at her hair, fanning it out in a golden-brown cloud, which she batted away from her face on a regular basis.

The path led them down to a weatherworn set of wooden steps, which deposited them on a crescent of beach. The salt-scented air was cold and pure like he imagined all the air was when God first made the world. He heard her suck in a breath as she took in the view. He did the same. He'd never lived near the beach until he'd bought the shop, and he took every opportunity he could to come and stare, just stare at the glory of the turbulent Pacific as it crashed against the black rocks of California's central coast.

The surf was particularly splendid today, he thought, sending up spirals of foam as it rolled in and out. The remnants of the storm had not entirely dissipated, so the clouds filtered the afternoon sunlight into soft yellow and white gold. As they watched, a pelican flew low over the water, its massive brown wings barely moving.

"Wow," she said.

"Yeah. Takes my breath away every time. You don't live along the coast?"

She continued to gaze at the ocean. Without her guardedness, she looked like an altogether different person. Fascinating. "No," she said faintly. "I live in San Francisco."

"Alone?"

She jerked toward him. Had he said that? Aloud? Yep, judging from her face, he really had. Now she thought he was a stalker. "I didn't mean to…" Way to go. Supersmart comment. He thought of the words in Job he'd listened to on the skippy cassette tape that morning while he dipped strawberries. *If only you would be altogether silent! For you, that would be wisdom.* Yeah, Job would say the same of him, no doubt. He rarely got into trouble when he was silent. Trouble was, he was rarely silent. Easy talk kept him afloat, kept people engaged in safe topics he could control. He used conversational sleight of hand to distract from other things.

While Bill considered what to say to undo the mess, he was saved from inserting his booted foot any further down his throat when he saw the blur of movement in the ice-plant-covered rocks along the cliff bottom.

Misty saw it too. Together they ran to the spot.

"Jellybean!" Misty called. "Where are you?"

A furry head popped up from above the plants.

"That was naughty to run away like that."

Jellybean wagged his tail.

"Where's Tinka?" she demanded. "What did you do with her?"

At the sound of her name, Tinka trotted from her hiding place, body quivering. Bill scooped her up. "Aww. Are you cold, little girl?" He tucked her inside his shirt. She burrowed against the warm skin of his stomach and pressed a chilled nose into his ribs. "One down, one to go."

"Jellybean," Misty said firmly. "Come."

Jellybean let out a bark but did not comply.

Misty repeated the command again and again but received only a blank stare from Jellybean.

"I think he's just pretending I'm not talking to him," she said, hands on hips.

"Not sure there's any pretending involved. Strong willed."

"Stubborn."

"Hardheaded?"

"Exasperating."

They could have been talking about Bill. "Do you want me to see if I can grab him?"

"Let me try one more time." She took two steps closer. "Jellybean, come here right now."

Jellybean's nose quivered, and he slithered out of the bushes, a pink flower caught in his long beard whiskers. Misty cooed as she bent over. "You really did come. I'm sorry I called you exasperating."

Just as her fingers grazed his fur, Jellybean wagged his tail and sprinted between Misty and Bill, beetling up the stairs in a blur of black.

Misty shot to her feet. "I take it back," she yelled to the departing dog. "You *are* exasperating."

∽

Misty and Bill finally decided to postpone the search and deliver Tinka back to Vivian. Back at the Lady Bird Hotel, Lawrence tried to offer the dog a welcome-home pat, but Vivian jerked the animal away from his reach.

"Lawrence, you leave my dog alone."

"I was just being kind," he said.

"You don't know how to be kind." Her words dripped with acid.

Lawrence sighed. "Maybe I've learned a thing or two."

"Old actor, tired old tricks," she said. "At least your being here has filled my hotel for the first time in ten years. I guess that's something." She turned her back on him and marched away.

Misty noted the expression in Lawrence's eyes as he watched Vivian depart. Something infinitely sad. Misty had decided it was impossible to decipher what was genuine emotion in Lawrence, but as he gazed at Vivian, grief shadowed his face.

Misty stood uncertainly. Should she offer comfort? Would it be construed as prying? Misty had never really understood, nor navigated well, the mysterious waters of social interaction. People were hard to read, unpredictable, and apt to turn away. Speech or silence? He saved her from the decision.

"Did you find my Jellybean?"

"No, I'm sorry, but I think he headed into town. I'll keep looking."

Lawrence sighed. "I'll return to the set to lie down and wait for word."

She noted that he did not offer to beat the sidewalks and help search.

The guests had done a question and answer with Lawrence and gobbled most of the chocolates, and Bill was busy gathering up his serving trays. He offered her a leftover sweet.

She blushed for no particular reason. "I'm okay."

He looked a bit crestfallen. "It's a salted caramel in dark chocolate. It's harder than you think to make a really good caramel.

You've got to melt the sugar and brown it without letting any crystallization happen."

At some point during the description, her mouth had begun to water. "Well, maybe one wouldn't hurt…since you worked so hard on it, I mean."

He brightened, green eyes sparkling. He didn't look much like a chocolatier—more like a cowboy with his broad shoulders, legs long and lean in denim jeans, and a thick thatch of brown hair that matched the slight stubble on his chin. Picking up a napkin, he retrieved a caramel and offered it to her.

She popped the treat into her mouth, and it melted into a puddle of bliss on her tongue. The symphony of flavors swamped her senses, the sweet of the chocolate and the salt from the caramel. "Amazing," she managed. "Did you go to a chocolatier school?"

He shrugged. "Nah. I learned from my mom, just informally, and taught myself the rest. It isn't what I thought my profession was going to be, but when I bought the place here in Albatross three months ago, Fee and I didn't need the whole building, so I set up a chocolate shop on the bottom floor. We opened unofficially a couple of weeks back."

"I'm surprised there isn't a line out your door."

His big smile made her nearly forget that he'd been nosy earlier. "Nice of you to say. It's been tough, actually. This is a small town, and the tourist trade is pretty slow in the winter. The only thing that's saved me is this movie thing going on. I'm counting on those tour buses rolling on in, and the locals are talking about hosting a Silver Screen Festival if you can believe it."

She eyed the empty table, wishing there was another stray chocolate she could somehow snag.

"How did you get hooked up with this movie deal?" Bill asked, holding the door open as they once again headed out in search of the elusive terrier.

"One of my online clients, Ernest Finn. He heard the film was

going to be shot here, and he knows a guy who arranges tutors for
the actors and gave him my name. He said he knew someone on
the set, so he was sure I could get the job."

"He didn't realize it was a dog sitting gig too."

She sighed. "Ernest meant well. He's a sweet man. I've been
teaching him violin for six years now. He lives just up the coast, I
think, though I've never met him face-to-face."

Bill looked puzzled. "You've known him for six years and never
met in person?"

Misty quickened her pace, feeling the blossoming urge to flee
that kicked up whenever she got into intimate conversation, especially with a handsome man, or any man for that matter. "It's better for me online."

"Why?" he said, catching up as they passed the Full of Beans
coffee shop.

"Why what?"

"Why is it better to teach online?"

She looked underneath the row of hydrangea bushes that lined
the sidewalk. "I can teach students all over the country, the world
even. I have a student in Africa."

"Huh. I guess that shouldn't surprise me. I've learned a ton of
things from YouTube. Just never knew you could learn to play an
instrument that way. Seems kind of lonely."

Lonely? She wasn't lonely. She had a life filled with siblings,
Nana Bett, and her students—the quiet life God meant for her to
live. The thoughtful twist to his brows made her think he wanted
to ask another question. "It's perfect for me."

She quickened her pace and pressed through the doors to
Hardware Emporium, a minuscule shop crowded with shelves of
everything from nuts and bolts to sheep food. The owner had not
seen an ill-behaved terrier slip by his doors.

Bill looked at his cell phone. "Almost one. I've gotta go pick
up Fiona. It's just down at the end of this street. You know, there's

a little park near her school with sand and stuff. Maybe Jellybean headed there. Want to walk that way and check it out?"

With him? She did not. People made her nervous, men made her nervous, men with genial smiles who wanted to ask personal questions especially. She'd loved one of those types before, and that wound hadn't healed. But with Lawrence's dog getting into who knew what, she could not figure out what to do except to follow Bill. The silence grew and became awkward, even for her. She should say something before he launched into any more conversation requiring her to share.

"How does your daughter like Albatross?"

"She's not my daughter, actually. She's my niece, my brother's only child. He and his wife, Bella, were killed in a car accident. There were no other relatives up for the job since my mother had a stroke awhile back and Bella's sister works overseas for an oil company. So she landed with me." He sighed. "Imagine that. I was the best pick." A shadow darkened his face. "Poor kid."

"Being raised in a chocolate shop doesn't sound so bad to me," she found herself saying. "It's like having Willy Wonka for a father."

"Who's that?"

"From the story about Charlie and his chocolate factory. Didn't you ever read that?"

He passed a hand over his forehead, and suddenly he appeared tired. Well, the man had been trailing a naughty dog all over town. "Nah, I must have missed that one."

They passed the park, which had several small children, parents, and dogs in attendance, but none of them was the AWOL Jellybean.

As they turned up the walkway to the preschool, Bill stopped so suddenly she plowed into him from behind.

"What's wrong?"

The sounds of cheerful piano music floated out from the school. Misty recognized the nursery song as one she taught her youngest

violin students. She couldn't imagine why the tune had such a pro-
found effect on Bill until she drew up next to him.

There, sitting on the "Welcome Friends" doormat, was Jellybean, who looked for all the world like a terrier with a smile on
his tiny face.

Four

Misty coaxed the annoying dog into her arms while Bill greeted Fiona. She looked up from her curled white paper festooned with splotches of blue, a tear in the middle where the paper had dissolved under the onslaught of too much paint. Her face lit up when she caught sight of him, and Bill felt all the cares of the day slide away as he hoisted her into the air. She waved goodbye to Miss Dina, who laid Fiona's masterpiece on a table to dry.

"Hey, big girl!" he said, whirling her around. "What did you do today?"

She grabbed hold of each of Bill's ears and pressed her forehead to his. He'd never understood the gesture, but it seemed to calm her. Having her slightly sticky fingers clasped around his ears, her cheek smudged with finger paint pressed close, calmed him as well.

"I see you painted. Was it fun?"

Fiona nodded.

"What did you have for snack time? Goldfish? Toast triangles? Apple slices?"

She remained silent, continuing to stroke his ears, looking sideways at Misty and Jellybean.

He realized Misty was staring at them. "Can you say hello to Ms. Agnelli and Jellybean?"

"She can call me Misty."

Misty looked at Fiona expectantly.

The seconds ticked by. Well, what had he imagined? That Fiona would suddenly launch into conversation with a stranger? But that's exactly what he did think, or hope anyway, that one day the door would open and all of Fiona's thoughts and feelings would gush out in a flood. It would be an incredible blessing…and scary as all get-out. What would he do with her feelings of loss and fear? How would he comfort her?

God would give him the words when He restored hers, he figured.

Bill let Fiona slide to the ground and took her hand while she smiled at Misty. Bill held his breath. Maybe this was it, the moment that would break through her walls of silence. Seconds ticked by until she wriggled her hand free and began picking up pebbles.

"She's not being rude, she…" He lowered his voice to a whisper. "The doctors said it's called selective mutism."

Misty's eyes widened.

"From the trauma of what happened."

"I'm sorry."

"It's okay." He noted that Fiona's shirt was stained with paint, and he wondered what was the proper laundry treatment for that. "She'll start talking again one day when she feels more secure." He frowned. "At least I hope so." Was her Uncle Bill enough to help her feel secure in the world? They walked along in silence, Jellybean wriggling to get down and Misty not allowing it.

"I'm delivering you to Lawrence," she told the dog, "and then you're his problem, not mine."

Bill looked at her. "Oh, are you still leaving, then?"

She nodded. "It's better that way. Mr. Tucker will find someone else to take care of his dog, and I'm available on Skype if he needs more music support. This whole movie thing was a mistake."

For some reason, Bill felt a pang of regret as they strolled along, eventually stopping outside Chocolate Heaven. "When will you leave?"

"Today. Tonight. As soon as I can."

He smiled. "We're that bad here in Albatross?"

"Yes. I mean no. Not you." She gripped the dog tighter. "Everyone's been nice. I just don't belong here."

"I felt that way too when I got here. I was working on a dude ranch in Klamath Falls when I heard about my brother. Never thought I'd be running a candy shop in Albatross. Figured I would be staying on that dude ranch till I was an old man. I loved it there—mountains, grassland, and plenty of horses." He paused. "So where do you belong?"

She froze, and he realized he'd been too personal again.

"Sorry. Not my business. I'm nosy, I know. I was just wondering…um…one lost soul to another. Where's your favorite place to hang out?"

She surprised him by answering, "My apartment. I don't like to venture out too much."

He thought he'd never heard anything so sad in his life. Inside four walls, teaching lessons over the computer.

"It's a great big world out there, Misty Agnelli," he said softly. "You never know what you might find if you look around."

She raised her chin, the sunlight painting her hair in caramel splendor. "I don't need to look around. I'm going home." She waved over the top of the whining dog. "Goodbye, Fiona. Thanks again, Mr. Woodson."

"Bill," he said to her departing back. "Please call me Bill."

But she was already too far away to hear.

With a sigh, he ushered Fiona inside.

The day passed in a blur. He snatched hours of prep time for the upcoming grand opening while Fiona colored with her fat crayons, this time everything in green. Gunther spent a while reading to her, and though he grumped about getting down on the floor, Bill noticed the man's angry, pinched look disappeared as he read something about a cow and a barn to Fiona. Gunther supervised her tricycle ride while Bill tended to the marshmallow cream filling for the Tucker's Treats he planned to push big-time when the tour bus rolled into town. The tours were scheduled every Friday for six weeks, and he did not intend to miss out on a single potential sale.

Seeing Gunther and Fiona together sent him drifting back to thoughts of his own family. His father had only recently sold his thriving veterinary practice because of his wife's precarious health. He hadn't seen much of his father in the last decade. The shouting match that occurred when Bill dropped out of high school halfway through his senior year echoed loud enough in his memory to carry through to the present.

"This is the dumbest thing you've ever done," his father hollered, slamming both palms on the table. "Anyone can get a diploma, even if you're not smart."

Even if you're not smart. And that was the bare bones of it. His father had always secretly wondered why his oldest son was dumb. Bill's younger brother, Dillon, was a computer engineer with a PhD in something technological, married to Bella, a CPA, with a fancy house in San Francisco. The Albatross property was to have been a summer home for the perfect couple and their little girl. Instead, their life insurance money secured the house for Uncle Bill and Fiona, the rest of their assets landing in a trust fund for their daughter to receive when she turned twenty-one.

His parents were still steeped in grief, but Bill knew deep down his father was thinking, *Why Dillon? The one who had his life together. The smart one.* Bill knew his father loved him and would never wish him harm, but in those dark, three a.m. moments when all the feelings he'd pushed away during the day rose up to attack him, he wondered the same thing: *God, why didn't You take the loser brother?*

Why didn't You take me?

The rich smell of chocolate roused him from his self-pity, and he mumbled a quick prayer. "I know You love me, God. I'm enough for You." If he could not teach Fiona anything else, he would teach her that. She would always know she was enough.

He looked up to find Fiona back in her pint-size chair, another book clutched in her hand, and Gunther pushing his glasses up on his nose. "She's a smart cookie."

His heart both thrilled and quavered at Gunther's pronouncement. Was this how parents felt? he wondered. All filled with hope that their children had just the right stuff to light up the world? It was a heady thought. He contemplated how far the fall must be when children could not live up to their parents' dreams, how bitterly it must have galled his own father, the smartest man he knew.

He gripped the spatula tighter. He would make a success of Chocolate Heaven by dint of hard work and excruciating hours, and he'd make sure Fiona had everything she could require, everything Dillon and Bella had wanted for her.

Would his father see Bill as a success then?

He turned back to the chocolate, soothing himself with creating the delicate shells that would be filled with mousse and topped with a tiny fondant bone and one jellybean—Jellybean Jumbles in honor of the feisty dog.

He was considering how to make chocolate violins to connect to the movie's theme when Gunther spoke up.

"Going home."

Bill was dismayed to find that it was after six. He'd not gotten nearly far enough.

"Okay. Thanks very much, Gunther. You're a natural with kids."

Gunther waved a gnarled hand. "Yeah, yeah. Lunk's enough for me."

Lunk was Gunther's couch potato mutt, an ottoman-sized bulldog mix.

Fiona waved goodbye to Gunther.

"Bath time for you, missy," Bill said.

After she'd finished her bath, eaten a plate of noodles, played building blocks, brushed her teeth, and done the final potty run, it was after seven. As he lay down on the floor beside her bed to listen to the story of the three little pigs on her CD player, he thought about the long list of things he needed to complete for the next day's grand opening.

The chocolate violins still twirled in his mind, and he decided to experiment after Fiona fell asleep. It was bad parenting, someone had told him, to stay with her while she drifted off to sleep. She was supposed to self-soothe or some such thing. He'd tried that precisely one time until he heard her sniffling into her blankets, her nose running and eyes swollen and still not crying aloud.

She should soothe herself? And how was she to know that the sun would rise in the morning, this child whose mommy and daddy were snatched away in an instant? How could she know there was nothing lurking in the darkness that would drag away her Uncle Bill too? From that night on, he'd lain on a blanket next to her bed, letting her fingers play with his hair until she slept, singing all the songs he could remember from his long-ago Sunday school.

Maybe he was making a mistake in soothing Fiona.

Wouldn't be the first time, he thought, as her chubby fingers found comfort twirling a lock of his hair. By the time she was grown, he would have made enough mistakes to fill up a book.

"Lord, help me," he mumbled as he too lost himself in sleep.

Misty stayed up late into the night, perched on a bench seat in her trailer as she scoured the Internet for local dog sitters. Jellybean had decided to make himself at home, and the creature was snoring under a bundle of covers. When she finally climbed into bed, she'd insisted he sleep on the floor, but sometime during the night he'd taken advantage of her unconscious state and invited himself aboard, tunneling under the blankets. There was something sweet, she thought for a moment, about a warm little dog all snuggled up next to a person.

"Remember, Jellybean is nothing but a bundle of trouble," she grumbled.

At the earliest hour that was decent, she began dialing. After a half dozen phone calls, she connected with a woman named Phyllis Marshall, who came with an impressive list of credentials on doggy behavior. Phyllis, to Misty's great delight, was stationed not a half hour away and promised to be on the set by ten to take charge of her fuzzy client.

Misty quietly packed her small bag. When Jellybean finally stuck his twitching nose up out of the covers, she clipped his collar to a leash.

"You're going to love Ms. Marshall," Misty said. "She's a dog expert. Practically a canine savant."

Jellybean stared in that vacant way of his. She took him outside to do his morning business and then offered a bowl of kibble. The dog looked from her to the food bowl in obvious disgust.

"Fine. We'll try later. Let's go find Lawrence."

The actor was poring over a script, coffee in one hand, a chocolate brioche in the other. Misty wondered if Bill had made the brioche, but she didn't know if he dabbled in pastry. *He might,* she thought. Something about his mixture of easy confidence, nosiness, and humility made him linger in her mind. Or maybe it was the courageous way he was attempting to raise a grieving little girl.

Her feelings of admiration for Bill were confusing. She remembered having similar thoughts about Jack—a man she had admired, respected, and grown to love. What a disaster that had turned out to be.

Lawrence was writing copious notes on his script, and he didn't seem to have a need for her musical tutelage. She started toward Mr. Wilson to explain about Phyllis's arrival and her own departure, but the man was whacking his baseball cap, complete with mayonnaise advertising and dog tooth holes, on his thigh, snarling at another man with a headset and clipboard. *Perhaps now is not the time*, she thought. When Phyllis arrived would be an altogether better moment.

Jellybean was dragging her away from the set, and she saw no reason not to follow his direction. She'd much rather take a quiet walk into town, enjoying the brisk sea air, than try to stay out of the way of cranky film people. At this early hour, she most likely would not run into anyone at all—the perfect scenario.

The town of Albatross was more alive than she'd ever seen it in the time of her short stay. Bill's shop sported a bouquet of colorful balloons outside, fastened to an easel offering everything from Tucker's Treats to Jellybean Jumbles. In the window she saw two delicate chocolate violins, each with a slender confectionary bow. How had the man done it? She was peering closer when Jellybean started to bark and yank the leash taut.

Fiona, her hand pressed to the inside of the glass door, looked out at them.

Misty tried to pull the dog away before he could attract any more attention, but it was too late. Bill, clad in jeans, a T-shirt that clung to his muscled torso, and a Chocolate Heaven apron, popped his head out the door. Fiona scooted past her uncle to scratch Jellybean's offered tummy.

"The violins," Misty blabbered, "they're awesome."

"Did I get it right?" His smile was wide and welcoming. "I looked at pictures in Fiona's storybook. There's one about a talking violin."

"They're perfect, right down to the tuning pegs." She looked past him and saw that the floor was sparkling. Additional bunches of balloons were tied on either side of the counter. Fiona was wearing a pink dress that tied at the waist and a bow in her neatly combed hair. "You're really pulling out all the stops for this grand opening."

"We have to. It's sink-or-swim time." He gestured her to come inside. "Let me get you a cup of coffee and a Close-Up Caramel." He gave her an elaborate wink. "Are you ready for your Close-Up, Misty Agnelli?"

She laughed. "You've been waiting all morning to say that, haven't you?"

He nodded. "Since I came up with the idea at two a.m."

"Thank you, but I can't. I'm just killing time until the new dog assistant arrives in"—she checked her watch—"about an hour."

"Might as well kill time with chocolate as anything else."

Something about his grin warmed her insides in a way she hadn't experienced since Jack. It made her nervous, more nervous than she usually felt when talking to strangers. The longer she hung around, the more awkward it would get.

"Thanks anyway," she said, trying to urge Jellybean to come along.

"You know," he said, "I've been thinking maybe Fiona should have violin lessons sometime. Is she old enough, do you think?"

"I recommend to most parents that they wait until age five."

"But Fiona's exceptional, I'm sure." A shadow passed across his bottle-green eyes. "Both her parents were musical. My brother played both the cello and the trumpet, actually."

"Do you play?"

"Me? No. My brother was the talented one."

Misty was more accomplished in terms of education and degrees than her five siblings, yet she understood exactly. Dating, marriages, friends—the normal social interactions of life—came easily to everyone in the Agnelli clan except Misty. They were a noisy, boisterous family who loved socializing, and she was the odd, awkward one. They loved her anyway.

The social anxiety had kicked in at age five after her father's accident, from which he had recovered and she had not. In one single moment, he had been struck by a distracted driver while walking the dog, and both their lives had changed forever.

"She'll grow out of it," her mother had said for years. She'd finally stopped saying it after her four younger brothers and sister had all gotten married, or at least engaged. Misty had barely even dated more than a dozen times. After she'd fallen in and out of love with Jack, her mother had come to accept that Misty was just not cut out of the same cloth. Misty had accepted it too. During her growing-up years, the doctors would hint at many causes for her oddities, social anxiety, and nonverbal learning disability, dyssemia, at which point Misty's mother would march out of the office. "No one is going to label you, Misty," she'd snap. "I won't allow it!"

Misty wondered sometimes if a label, a name for the strangeness that set her apart from her own noisy clan, would have made her life easier. In any case, she was who she was, who God created her to be. He had made her to speak through her music, and that was usually sufficient.

But just now, standing awkwardly opposite an extremely intriguing and not at all bad-looking man, she wished for a brief moment that she were more like her siblings. The rumble of a motor made them turn. A tour bus rolled past. "Everybody smile and wave," Bill said.

The three of them did just that, earning several return waves from the people crammed on the bus. "Looks full," Misty said.

"Sure does," Bill said, straightening his apron. "They'll be coming here after their stop at the film set. Do you want to stick around for the fun?"

"I hope they do, Bill. I'd better get back to the set. Lawrence will want to show off Jellybean. He says everyone loves a celebrity dog."

"Maybe Fiona and I will sneak up too. Everything here is ready."

"Okay," she said. "You're welcome in my trailer." She felt her face go scarlet. "I meant…you know, if Fiona needed a bathroom or a drink of water or anything."

He smiled. "I knew what you meant. Maybe I'll see you there."

"Well, uh, depends on the timing. I'm leaving at lunch."

"That soon?" Bill said.

Did she detect a look of disappointment on his face?

Surely not. People were not generally disappointed to see her go. Relieved, usually, but not disappointed. She waved goodbye to Fiona. In the distance, the tour bus churned away in a cloud of exhaust.

I hope it goes well for you, Bill Woodson, she said silently, resisting the urge to look back.

Five

Misty hightailed it to the grassy field that was home to the film shoot, making it back as the bus slowed to a stop. A gentleman with a black mustache and a clipboard hopped out first. The name tag clipped to his lapel read "Tom" with a little smiley face inside the *o*.

"Here, ladies and gentlemen," he called out, ushering them to find a seat in a cluster of folding chairs arranged between Misty's trailer and the one that was home to the director. A woman wearing a pink hat waved madly at Misty. No doubt she was a Jellybean fan.

Drat, Misty thought, wiggling her fingers in a halfhearted response. The tourists were blocking access to her door. She'd been hoping to hand Jellybean off to Lawrence, hole up in her trailer, and avoid the crowd until Ms. Marshall arrived. Now a new flood of people turned their interest in her direction. Her skin erupted in cold prickles. As she began a backward creep away from the assembled tourists, Lawrence swept into view, greeting the delighted group with hearty affirmations. Strolling by, he beamed at Misty, patted her shoulder, and gathered up a wriggling Jellybean.

Relieved and edging to the back of the group, Misty watched in awe as Lawrence worked the crowd of sixty or so starstruck visitors. "Welcome to the battlefield," he chortled, sweeping a hand toward the Sherman tank. The top hatch of the tank was open, and a uniformed actor was manning the machine gun. He waved, and the tourists captured it all with their cell phone cameras before the actor climbed out and joined the presentation.

Misty continued to ease toward the periphery, and by the time she'd neared the spot where the tour bus was parked, Bill and Fiona were just strolling up. Her heart jumped oddly, and after a moment she forced a jerky wave.

Bill waved back, and Fiona smiled around the two fingers jammed in her mouth.

"This is quite a crowd," Bill said, eyes sparkling.

"Lots of people hungry for chocolate."

He laughed. It was a warm, comforting sound. She must have said the right thing.

"It sounds so opportunistic, but yeah, that's what I was hoping for. Maybe some of them will stay the night at the inn and pop into the diner and the gift shop. Good for the whole town."

It was hard not to notice how his eyes sparkled when he talked, his big hands cuddling Fiona to his side. It was one of those times she desperately wished she had the gift of gab, a grasp of the easy social give-and-take that was so natural for some folks. *How do they do it?* she wondered. *Let the conversation flow like the notes in a concerto?* The only thing she knew how to talk about without the least hesitation was music, but she did not see how to wedge that topic into the present situation.

As she tried to think of something else to say, another vehicle rolled into a graveled section of the field that provided a makeshift parking lot.

A white van with "Well-Heeled Hound" lettered on the side stopped behind the bus. A woman wearing neat trousers and a button-up canvas shirt with a tiny dog emblem on the pocket stepped out. Her long blond hair was coiled in a neat braid that wound around her head, and she wore sporty glasses with red frames. Every inch of Phyllis Marshall said, "I can handle Jellybean. No sweat."

Misty exhaled in relief and hastened to extend her hand and introduce herself.

With a firm grip, Phyllis shook Misty's palm. "Where's my little gentleman?"

It took Misty a beat to figure out she was referring to Jellybean. "Oh, um, he's over there."

Phyllis looked closely at Jellybean. "Wire-haired terrier with a touch of something else?" Phyllis inquired. "Cairn terrier, perhaps?"

Misty thought maybe it was a touch of mule, but she didn't have the courage to say so.

Lawrence had started the group off on a walk, and they were now milling around the tank. Jellybean thrashed wildly in Lawrence's arms in an effort to be set free.

"Ah," Phyllis said, marching toward Jellybean and the crowd.

Misty returned to Bill and Fiona. "I can't wait to see how she handles Jellybean," Misty said.

"I can't wait to see how she handles Lawrence," Bill replied.

Misty hadn't thought of that. She hoped the woman was a cinema fan, awed to be in the very presence of the great actor like everyone else appeared to be. Somehow, Phyllis didn't look to be the type who was easily awed by anything.

They moved closer toward the collected audience. Lawrence was looking down his nose at Phyllis, who had picked her way to the front and must have introduced herself.

"So you're a dog trainer?" Lawrence sniffed. "Thank you for your interest, but Jellybean doesn't need training. He just needs supervision."

Misty didn't know if Lawrence was lying or if he actually believed his own lines.

Jellybean finally wriggled loose from Lawrence's grip and hopped to the ground. Phyllis beamed, fished a teensy brown dog treat from her pocket, and held it toward Jellybean. The dog's nose quivered.

"Sit, Jellybean."

The dog sat. He was given the treat.

Misty gaped.

"See?" Lawrence said as if he'd been expecting such behavior. "He's already trained." The guy really must be a fine actor.

"Good," Phyllis said calmly. "Down," she said, bending to hold the treat on the grass, and Jellybean followed her movements, lying on the ground, resting his wedge of a head on dainty paws. His pink tongue snaked out to snag the treat.

"Did you see that?" Misty whispered to Bill.

Bill nodded, hoisting Fiona on his broad shoulders so she could get a better view. "She's a canine genius."

Phyllis offered Lawrence a cool smile. "Come, Jellybean." Out came another dog treat, and after a moment Jellybean sat up, padding directly to Phyllis.

Misty looked closer to be sure no one had replaced Jellybean with a stunt double. Nope, it appeared to be the same feisty terrier who was now behaving like a blue ribbon champion.

"We'll work on making that a bit faster," she said, giving Jellybean a pat on the head. "Eventually, he'll comply without the need for a tangible reward." She took a blue lead from her seemingly bottomless pockets. "Time to put you on the leash, Jellybean. Sit."

She held the treat in front of Jellybean's nose. The enticing aroma brought him right to a textbook sit. Whatever these dog treats were made from, Misty figured it had to be like doggy catnip or something. She wondered if it would work on some of her wiggly students as well.

Smiling, Phyllis held the treat a bit away from Jellybean while she bent over to clip the leash to his collar. With a blur of motion,

Jellybean snapped the treat from her hand and zoomed away a few paces out of reach.

"Uh-oh," Bill said.

A slight frown crossed Phyllis's face. She cast a withering look at Lawrence. "He does need basic training."

Lawrence sniffed. "He is merely pointing out that he can't be bought with paltry dog treats."

Phyllis ignored him, turning again to Jellybean, who was crouched low in the front and high in the rear, tail wagging. The tourists were now watching the proceedings with rapt attention. Phyllis bent again, keeping the treat tighter between her fingertips.

"Jellybean, come."

This time the dog sprang forward so unexpectedly, Phyllis toppled over on her bottom. Jellybean scarfed the fallen treat and skittered a few paces away, tail whirling in happy circles.

"Bad dog," Phyllis hissed.

To Misty's horror, Lawrence started laughing.

"I believe he's bested you, Dog Trainer Phyllis," he chortled. Misty hurried to offer Phyllis a hand up, but the woman waved her off and got to her feet.

The confused audience looked from Lawrence to Phyllis as the two stared at each other.

She fingered another treat. "Come, Jellybean."

The dog came close, and Misty thought she saw a nasty gleam in the terrier's eye.

"Uh…" Misty started.

Phyllis bent, leash in one palm and treat in the other.

"Maybe…" Misty tried.

"Come," Phyllis repeated.

This time Jellybean came and sat as requested, allowing Phyllis to clip on the leash.

Misty blinked in disbelief at Jellybean, suddenly an angel in a fur coat, as he came closer, ears cocked and button nose quivering.

By this time the director had arrived on scene, baseball cap firmly in place. "Check that out," he said, beaming. "That's exactly what we need for the animal. Some good, no-nonsense training." He hastened to Phyllis. "Can you take him to your dog compound for some boot camp? He needs massive rehearsal."

Lawrence glared at the director. "As I have already explained, I don't work on a set without Jellybean."

Phyllis stood with the leash in hand, her attention on Wilson. "I will be happy to come during the shoot hours. You'll see amazing progress by the end of the week."

Misty stared at Jellybean. It was almost as if she could see him considering, gauging the optimal timing, waiting for the perfect cue. He turned his bright black eyes on Misty and smiled. No, she must have imagined that. Dogs didn't really smile, did they?

"Mr. Tucker, shall we discuss my fee?" Phyllis said.

And then the dog put his plan into action. Exploding into motion, he ran between Phyllis's legs and circled back, tangling the leash around both ankles. When the leash pulled taut, she stumbled and lost her grip, dropping some doggy treats on the ground. Jellybean zoomed in, scarfed the treats, and rocketed away.

Now free with the leash trailing behind him, Jellybean dashed toward the tank, scrambled up the turret, and disappeared into the metal bowels.

A collective gasp rose from the crowd, many of whom were videoing the proceedings on their cell phones.

"Look at that," one man guffawed. "The dog is prepared to battle it out."

But no one was laughing harder than Lawrence.

Bill gaped. He didn't know much about movies and even less about dog training, but he was absolutely certain that laughing at a woman—any woman—in front of a crowd or not was generally a very bad idea.

Lawrence had tears of mirth running down his face.

Phyllis had something akin to steam shooting out of her ears, or so Bill imagined.

From her position on his shoulders, Fiona must have felt the tension too, because she reached down and cupped his cheeks. He patted her chubby fingers to reassure her.

Misty's complexion had gone from a mild pink to a dead white. Bill understood. Phyllis, Misty's ticket out of town, stood with her hands fisted on her hips. Another bad sign in the world of women.

The guy Bill knew to be the director stepped forward. "Mr. Tucker, this is inappropriate and disrespectful. This lady has come to help train your incorrigible beast."

Lawrence turned cold eyes on Wilson. "Sir, I do not appreciate such slander."

"Time to call a spade a spade, Tucker."

Lawrence considered and then waved his hand airily. "Fine. Go ahead and fish him out of the tank for Dog Trainer Phyllis."

"He's your mutt," Wilson snapped. "You do it."

"I don't like your tone, Director," Lawrence said. "I told you I did not require a dog trainer."

"Yes, you do. Unless you've forgotten, your dog just commandeered a Sherman tank!" the director thundered.

"Well, kudos to him," Lawrence shouted back. "He didn't ask to be harassed by some dog warden."

The director's mouth tightened. "Mr. Tucker," he said through gritted teeth, "these people—all of these lovely visitors, who will someday be paying to see this movie—are not here to witness you have a temper tantrum."

The tour director, Tom, nodded vigorously.

"Oh, don't stop on our account," a heavyset man said, hoisting a camera loaded with lenses. "This is a whole lot more fun than some canned speech."

Bill had to agree until he caught a glimpse of Misty's stricken face.

He put a hand on her shoulder.

She turned wide eyes on him. "This is all my fault," she mouthed.

"Don't beat yourself up about it," Bill whispered. "Jellybean and Lawrence both need some training,"

A hollow bark echoed from inside the tank. The crowd hooted with laughter.

"Your dog is incorrigible," Phyllis said. "But at least dogs can be trained."

Lawrence shot a look at Phyllis. "He outflanked his opponent. It was a worthy effort from a creature who is not going to be tamed by paltry dog kibbles or whatever those treats are you keep plying him with, so you can leave and return to your doggy prison yard."

Phyllis stiffened with rage.

Tom the tour guide's mouth dropped open. "Uh, ladies and gentlemen," he said to the crowd, "perhaps we'd better delay our visit to Albatross until a later time."

"No need for them to leave," Phyllis snapped. "I'm going."

"You do that," Lawrence said.

"Wait," Misty tried. "I'm so sorry, Phyllis. This is just a bad time. Maybe we can try again later."

Jellybean barked again from inside the tank.

"I will not work for a man like that," Phyllis spat, disdain dripping from her words as she spun on her heel and stalked away.

"You see?" Lawrence said. "She doesn't want to stay. Misty, you will have to take care of Jellybean."

Misty finally got her mouth working. "No, I don't. I'm leaving."

Wilson's face was still flushed with anger. "Tucker, you've got to go catch up with that dog trainer," he said, pointing a finger at

Lawrence, "because your monster pet is not going to live in my Sherman tank."

"Don't worry," Lawrence said, eyes narrowed. "Jellybean will come out of your precious tank when he's good and ready, and then we are both leaving."

"No, you aren't. You can't walk off this set."

Lawrence pulled himself up to his full height and delivered what could have been a line straight from one of his movies. "I can, Director Wilson, and I will." Lawrence stalked to his trailer, plowed inside, and slammed the door.

Wilson slapped his hat against his thigh. An assistant ran up, and Wilson shouldered him aside, stalking to his own trailer and slamming the door.

After a moment of confusion, Tom made flapping motions with his hands as his tour group broke into a frenzy of conversation.

"Please return to the bus," Tom said in a high-pitched voice, but no one seemed to be listening to him.

Misty stood frozen to the spot. Bill was not sure what he could do. He wondered how a dog no bigger than a loaf of bread had accomplished so much damage in a matter of moments. His bigger problem was that the whole batch of potential customers was about to pile back onto the bus and leave town without purchasing so much as one measly Jellybean Jumble.

"We've got plenty of great stores in town," he called out to Tom. "And an amazing chocolate shop. You don't want to miss that."

Tom glowered at him. "There's nothing amazing about this hick town," he sneered.

Hick town? Bill was about to give Tom a piece of his mind. Misty was jogging after Phyllis, calling for her to wait.

Phyllis sailed on.

At that moment, Jellybean popped his head out of the hatch and barked, looking for all the world like a soldier who had just vanquished the enemy.

Six

Phyllis didn't actually refuse Misty's plea. She simply got into her car, shut the door, and motored off.

Breathing hard, Misty tried to think rationally. So the Phyllis thing hadn't worked out. That didn't mean Misty had to stay. She'd never signed a doggy care contract. Her music tutoring obligation was met. She could leave in good conscience.

But her conscience was doing the rhumba. Lawrence had just quit the movie because she'd forced a confrontation by bringing Phyllis along. How was she going to fix that? She had to do something fast before the tourists made for the bus. As she regarded the swarming visitors, her stomach clenched. The last thing she wanted to do was rejoin that milling crowd of people, but there was no other way. Mumbling a prayer that God would help her fix the disaster she'd just created, she jogged back just in time to find Tom corralling his tourists.

"Change of plans," he said. "We're going to head up the coast to Half Moon Bay. There's some great shopping there."

"Oh, don't do that," she said. "I'm sure Mr. Tucker will come out in a minute. You won't want your group to miss him or their visit to Albatross. It's so quaint."

Tom's brows knitted together in a frown, his voice low. "Listen, lady. The only reason I stopped at this Podunk town was to see a movie star. No star, no stay." He straightened. "All right, everyone. Back to the bus," he chirped.

Misty looked quickly, hoping Bill hadn't overheard the Podunk town comment, but he was standing amid a sea of tourists, Fiona still on his shoulders. She thought about the chocolate violins and the balloons decorating the front window of the chocolate shop. All that work and expense for nothing. She wanted to leap behind the wheel of the bus and drive them all back to town whether they wanted to go or not, but her feet were rooted to the spot.

There was only one option. She had to convince Lawrence to quit his pouting and greet his public before they all left. "Give me a minute. I'm sure I can persuade him to come out."

Hurrying to his trailer door, she knocked.

"Mr.…I mean Lawrence, you have to open the door. Your fans are waiting to see you."

Nothing.

She pounded harder. "Please, Lawrence. I'm sorry I brought Phyllis here, but there are people counting on you."

Still no sound of movement. Anger simmered in her veins. If she, Misty Agnelli, could face this mob of uncertainty, surely a seasoned actor could pull himself together enough to do a meet and greet. What happened to that "time to let it shine" philosophy?

She was about to pound for the third time when she felt a hand on her back. She whirled to see the tiny lady in a pink hat, only now she got a good look at the age-spotted face underneath the brim.

"Nana?" she managed.

Her grandmother beamed. "Well, look at you here, Misty Agnelli. My sweet granddaughter running things on a film set."

Conflicting emotions zigzagged through her insides as she wrapped Nana Bett, slippery in her pink raincoat, in a tight hug. "What are you doing here?"

"Didn't you see me waving earlier? I'm on the tour to see Lawrence Tucker." Her expression grew reverent as she put a hand to the trailer door. "Imagine being this close to him."

"Did you see what just happened, Nana? He had a fight with the director, and he quit the film."

She clamped on her pink hat to keep the breeze from taking it. "Oh, that was merely some drama served up for our benefit. He wouldn't really quit. Cinema is his life."

"But his dog..."

She laughed merrily. "I saw that. An absolute hoot. I haven't laughed so hard in years." Her eyes sparkled, and Misty noticed a healthy flush on her cheeks. "So," she said, voice dropping conspiratorially. "What's it like to be his assistant?" She gave Misty's chin a pinch. "I'm so proud of you—being here with all these people around. I know it must be tricky, but you're obviously doing great."

No one had a better picture of Misty's difficulties than her nana, but this time the woman was way off.

"Actually..."

"This is the very thing I've been praying would happen, Misty," she said, squeezing Misty's hand. "God's given you that little push to step out into the world. And here you are."

Here I am, she thought. With a movie star locked in his trailer, a dog hunkered in the belly of a Sherman tank, and tourists streaming back onto the bus, leaving behind a store full of chocolates.

Tom bustled over. "Ms. Agnelli, the bus is leaving now. Please take your seat."

"Thank you, Tom, but I'll find my own way home."

He frowned. "You've paid for a seat. It's not refundable."

"Nana," Misty started. Her grandma was on a fixed income. Rather than reside with the Agnelli family in Sausalito, Nana lived in a tiny apartment in a retirement community in Berkeley, the city she'd adored for a lifetime. The Agnellis did their best to make sure she had some nice-to-haves, but Nana was a proud person who always insisted on paying her own way. She would have had to save to afford a bus tour.

Nana held up a hand. "Tom, this is my granddaughter, Misty Agnelli. She works on the film as Mr. Tucker's assistant."

Tom looked sympathetically at Nana. "I'm sure she'll find another job." And then he spun on his heel and walked away.

"What is he talking about?" Nana said. "Mr. Tucker is having a short time-out, that's all. He's a professional."

"Nana…" Misty started again.

An actor wearing fatigues, a helmet, knee pads, and elbow pads and holding a broom waddled into view.

Nana stared. "What's he supposed to be?" she whispered.

The man paused to straighten his helmet and then staggered toward the tank. Misty remembered his name was Larry.

"What are you doing, Larry?" Misty asked, a worrisome thought taking root.

"Wilson says I'm to get that dog out of the tank."

"Oh, he'll come out when he's hungry," she said hastily. "There's no need for drastic measures."

"The director said if I don't get that dog out of that tank in ten minutes, he's calling the police."

The police? What exactly were they supposed to do? Send in a SWAT team?

Larry readied his broomstick and approached the tank.

"You aren't going to hurt Jellybean, right?" Misty called.

"Hurt him? That dog nipped me right in the rear yesterday. This broomstick is for my own protection."

Bill joined in, Fiona still on his shoulders. Misty introduced them to Nana Bett.

Fiona regarded the granny in pink with a shy smile.

"You know, I am sure I have a lollipop here in my purse. Let me look." She began to rummage through her cavernous bag. Misty smiled. Nana was constantly picking up freebies from the bank and doctors' offices. "In case I find someone who needs a blessing," she would say.

Bill tracked Larry's progress as he climbed toward the turret.

"How about if you open the escape hatch?" Bill called.

"How's that?" Larry said, struggling to climb while holding on to the broomstick.

"The escape hatch." Bill pointed. "It's on the bottom. Maybe Jellybean will climb out on his own."

Nana Bett momentarily stopped her rummaging. "Well, aren't you clever to know about that."

Bill chuckled. "Saw it on a TV program one time."

"Clever," Nana said. Misty thought there was a calculating arch to her brow.

Don't get any ideas, she wanted to say. *I'm. Leaving. This. Town. Immediately.*

Larry nodded. "Oh, yeah. Good idea."

Bill put Fiona down next to Nana Bett, who produced a red lollipop and pulled off the plastic. "Here you go, sweetie. I knew I had a treat in here for such a darling girl."

Fiona took the candy and put it in her mouth while Bill crawled under the tank and waited for Larry to burrow down inside. Together they opened the escape hatch. Larry popped his head out of the hole.

"No sign of Jellybean, but I'm— Ouch!" he hollered. "It's a surprise attack!" What followed was a loud clanking and rattling, a series of angry invectives, and one ominous clang. Larry scrambled out the escape hatch, his helmet askew, rubbing his shoulder.

"That's it," he yelled, throwing the helmet on the ground. "I don't care if they have to send in the seventh fleet to get that mutt. He's not biting me in the buns anymore, do you hear?"

Larry shook his fist at no one in particular and stomped away.

Misty had a sudden flash of inspiration.

She turned to her trailer. "Be back in a minute, Nana." She returned with the violin. Standing close to the tank, she played the second movement of Mozart's Fifth Violin Concerto.

Bill, Fiona, and Nana Bett stared at her. She didn't have time to explain the dog's strange fascination with music. It took no more than twenty measures for a wee canine head to peek cautiously out of the hatch.

"Come on out, Jellybean," she said, still playing softly. "It's time to end this skirmish."

After another few bars, Jellybean slithered out, sitting under the body of the tank, listening with rapt attention.

"Bravo, Misty," Bill called.

Part of her thrilled to hear him say it.

She stopped playing, transferred the bow and violin to one hand, and bent to grab Jellybean's leash with the other.

With a quick swish of his tail, Jellybean shot from under the tank and beelined across the field, headed toward town.

Misty groaned. Not again. She handed the instrument to her grandmother and took off in pursuit.

"See that?" she heard Nana say as she raced away. "Misty is taking care of everything."

∽

Bill wanted to sprint after Misty, but he couldn't leave Nana Bett and Fiona behind. Nana was eyeing him closely.

"So you're a friend of Misty's?" she asked.

"Yes. We just met two days ago." He laughed. "Ironically, she showed up at my store looking for Jellybean." He told her about his chocolate shop and his imperiled plans for a "grand opening," trying not to let his disappointment show.

"Oh, I see," she said. "And all your customers just drove away in the tour bus, didn't they?"

He sighed. "Yeah."

She pursed her lips. "You know, Bill, my husband, Nigel, was a singer and dancer. He was a smash eventually, but sometimes during the early years of our marriage, he would show up to perform and there would be no one there. Not a soul. You know what he did?"

"No, ma'am."

"He sang and danced for the janitor or the cook, anyone in the building. 'Never waste a stage,' he'd say."

"Sounds like quite a man."

"He was. He was a brilliant entertainer, and he even did some movie work. Just when he really hit the big time, he was thrown from a horse and became a paraplegic."

"I'm sorry."

"There was a silver lining. The accident changed both our lives in ways we could never imagine and introduced us both to Jesus." She winked. "I'll tell you more about it sometime."

Bill looked down at the tiny woman with the sparkling eyes and the jaunty pink hat. "Ma'am, I would love to hear more about your husband. Would you care to go to town and enjoy some premium chocolates while I help Misty find that dog?"

She crooked her arm in his. "I would be delighted, sir. Lead on."

Bill found Larry, who was applying a carefully placed ice pack, and told him he needed some transportation. Then he helped himself to one of the three golf carts that sat idle outside Larry's trailer. It didn't seem like anyone would be inconvenienced if he borrowed one for a while. Besides, he was technically on movie business since they were going to assist in tracking down the star's dog. He helped Nana Bett aboard and sandwiched Fiona between the two of them.

Fiona bounced up and down with excitement, and he had to admit, zooming along in the golf cart was more fun than he'd had in a long time. It wasn't quite the same as riding horseback down a mountain trail, but it was close. Nana Bett clapped her hat on with one hand and chortled with every bump and lurch, which made him seek out all the divots he could. There was no sign of Misty as they traversed the mile and a half back to town. She must have peeled off toward the beach or behind the hotel. He figured he'd get Nana settled in the chocolate shop with Gunther and head out to find Misty.

When they arrived at Chocolate Heaven, Gunther was sitting in a folding chair on the porch in a pool of sunshine, dozing. The balloons drifted in the wind, softly bonking him on the head.

"Minding the shop, I see," Bill said.

Gunther opened one eye and yawned. "Nothing to mind. What happened to all these tourists we've been killing ourselves over?"

Bill shook his head. "They skipped town."

"All except this one," Nana Bett said, stepping forward and extending her hand. "I'm Bett Agnelli. I'm here to see this amazing chocolate."

Gunther shook her hand. "Might as well. Isn't exactly a crowd here today." He led them into the shop and showed Bett the sweets in the glass case. "And this one here's filled with dark chocolate mousse."

Nana Bett exclaimed over each and every confection. Gunther warmed to his topic. "And that there is kind of a combo, you see, with the milk chocolate and the dark. Let me get you one to try."

While she sat at a table and Gunther offered one treat after another, Fiona crept closer, book in hand.

Nana looked over. "Would you like me to read to you, Miss Fiona?"

Fiona looked down, suddenly shy.

"She doesn't talk, but I know she would love a story," Bill said.

Nana nodded. "I thought she was pretty quiet. When Misty

was five, her daddy had a bad car accident, and Misty took it very hard. It was difficult to get her to say anything either."

Bill wondered if that had kick-started Misty's anxiety.

Bett confirmed his suspicion with her next words. "All that fear about her daddy sort of got stuck inside her, took away her confidence. She was always a shy child anyway, but after that…" Bett sighed. "Well, she had to be coaxed from the house. Still does."

Fiona climbed up.

Nana Bett launched into the pig and the pony story, rendering every page with gusto. As Bill grabbed a jacket in preparation to help with the Jellybean search, he tried to listen closely so he could tell Fiona the story just the same way later when the child inevitably would want it of him. Nana Bett was a natural storyteller, and he knew he couldn't do her rendition justice. Maybe he could get her to record it before she left.

As he seized the door to open it, Misty appeared, hair tousled and cheeks red.

"Hey," Bill said.

"Hi." She sucked in a breath and caught sight of her grandmother. "Oh, hi, Nana. How did you get here?"

"I had a thrilling ride in a golf cart with Bill and Fiona," she said. "And now I'm stuffing myself full of chocolates and storybooks. Best day ever. Did you find Jellybean?"

"No," Misty answered. "But I found this guy."

A big dog waddled into the shop, panting hard, tongue unfurled like a fluttering flag.

Gunther did a double take. "Lunk? Just how did you get out this time?"

"I found him behind the hotel. Vivian said he was yours. He got into the garbage can and was eating dill pickles and a baguette."

"A baguette?" Gunther snorted, grimacing at his dog. "You didn't hear the doc say you're getting chubby?"

Lunk licked his rubbery lips and collapsed with a wheeze onto the floor, immediately settling into a doze. "He's become a regular Houdini the past few months."

The phone rang, and Bill snatched it up. "Hello?" He listened to the ranting for a moment. "I understand. We'll be right over." He hung up.

"What?" Misty said, trying to read his expression. "You have a funny look. I can't tell if it's good news or bad."

"That was Vivian Buckley over at the hotel. She says she knows where you can find Jellybean, and he'd better stay away from her Tinka."

Gunther rubbed a hand over his cheeks. "This town is going to the dogs."

"Literally," Bill said.

Seven

Nana Bett had opted to stay in the shop and keep an eye on things while Gunther took Lunk back home and Misty, Bill, and Fiona headed to the Lady Bird.

"I used to run the till for a soda shop when I was a teen. It can't have changed that much," Nana said.

Misty was surprised to find she was right. Bill used an ancient cash register, which sat on the counter like a relic from a bygone age. He must have a device somewhere for taking credit cards. The idea of manually accepting money and making change seemed archaic. Didn't he realize that payments could be done electronically now? She hadn't set foot in her bank in a decade, and that was just fine by her. "Better to live through technology" was Misty's motto.

With Nana installed behind the counter wearing a paper Chocolate Heaven hat, her head barely showing over the dinosaur of a cash register, they started for the hotel. Fiona stayed close to Bill, sucking on her red lollipop. Vivian met them in front, Tinka cradled in her arms.

"Of course the dog is incorrigible," Vivian said, as if they arrived smack-dab in the middle of some sort of diatribe. "Look at the owner."

Misty figured a direct approach was best. "Where's Jellybean?"

Vivian's eyes narrowed, cheeks framed by tendrils of hair that frizzed out from her braid. "Tinka's been lethargic, so I thought some fresh air might help. I was walking her on the trail that borders the field where the film is shooting. It wasn't because I wanted to see Lawrence or anyone else, of course. That's just our route."

"But where's…" Misty started again.

"I'm not going to change things because of some celebrity visitors, even the high-and-mighty Lawrence Tucker." She stroked the dog, running her fingers through her silky hair. "He might as well live in a castle now, but I'll always know he's just a foster kid from Fresno, and he can't pretend that away as much as he tries." Tinka licked her owner's chin, and Vivian cuddled her close. "Acting is lying for a living, and Lawrence can't recognize the truth anymore."

"Vivian!" Misty said so loudly that the woman jumped. "Where's Jellybean?"

She blinked. "As I said, I was walking along the field, and that horrible dog ran up, leash trailing. I shooed him away, even shouted at him, but he would not leave us alone. What choice did I have really?" She shook her head. "Lawrence never gave me choices. It was love me or don't, but he was never the one who had to sacrifice."

Misty opened her mouth to vent the frustration building in her belly when Bill stopped her with a hand on her forearm. She couldn't fully interpret his expression, but she'd seen it before, and she knew it probably meant "Stop talking." So she did.

Bill smiled at Vivian. "Lawrence is a piece of work, for sure. So Jellybean wouldn't leave you and Tinka alone? So you did what with him exactly?"

"Took him to Lawrence's trailer. I banged on that door for ten

minutes. Lawrence shouted that he wasn't coming out, that he
needed time to center himself or some such drivel. I hollered loud
enough to wake the dead. I told him to put on his big-boy, real-
world pants and come get his disgusting dog, but he refused to
open the door. Can you believe that?"

Misty could. Who wouldn't want to stay in a nice, quiet trailer
when a lady was hollering just outside the door?

"And you brought Jellybean back here," Bill prompted.

"No."

Misty could feel all her life juices turning to steam. Again, Bill
squeezed her forearm.

"Then where's the dog, Vivian?" he said.

"I tied him to the door of Lawrence's trailer. Then I came back
and called you."

Misty exhaled her tension in a big whoosh of air. Without
another word, she about-faced to start the long walk back to Lawrence's trailer.

"How about we take the golf cart?" Bill said when he caught
up to her.

She thought about it. Riding next to him meant making small
talk, an activity that pained her. Finally, after struggling during
the course of her relationship with Jack, she'd learned that small
talk was invented merely to pass the time, and letting the conversation drift from topic to topic without reaching a specific answer
or conclusion was okay. She'd always be grateful to Jack for helping her reach that epiphany. Still, she wasn't good at it, and it was
even harder when a handsome man was involved. "Um...I should
walk. Good exercise."

"You've had enough exercise. Let me drive you." He gave her
a wink. "I'll just chitchat, and you don't have to chime in. How
about that?"

She started. How did he know? The wink would indicate a
joke, but what if he really meant he would do all the talking and

she could just listen? What would it be like simply to stay quiet and listen to the talk of the man with the electric eyes and boyish grin?

"Actually, this isn't a hard decision. Come on." He took Fiona's hand again, and they walked back to the shop. Gunther had returned, and he and Nana Bett were chatting, so Bill filled them in before he guided Fiona and Misty into the golf cart.

Bill did indeed shoulder the whole conversation back to the field, she was delighted to discover.

"Vivian and Lawrence sure have some kind of prickly past," he said in between giggles from Fiona as they hit a pothole that Misty suspected he had intentionally aimed for. He nodded conspiratorially at Misty. "Giggles are the only sound she makes, so I like to hear them."

To hear them and, she suspected, to savor the sounds as if they were precious notes strung together. She remembered the first time her father had spoken after the tubes were finally removed, the frightening machines rolled away. The light of recognition in his eyes funneled into the one joyful syllable: "Here."

I'm here. God brought me back. I love you. She'd heard it all in that single precious sound.

"Wonder what happened between Lawrence and Vivian." Bill shot her a glance. "I know, not my concern. My mom tells me I should mind my own business, but being curious is the only way I've learned things in my life. Everything from how to reassemble an engine to the best way to chocolate dip a strawberry." He laughed. "I guess curiosity is a good thing, to a degree."

She concurred. Curiosity—that burning desire to know everything about the violin—had fallen on her like burning ash, lighting a passion inside that was still as bright as it was when she was eight years old. Misty Agnelli was not sure of many things in her life, but she knew without a doubt that God meant for her to love the violin.

Listening to Bill was akin to playing a light and airy melody.

His words danced along like her bow on the strings, unfettered by her own awkward conversational contributions. How sweet just to listen without the tension of having to reply.

"You know," he said, "no pressure, but if you have something to say, I'm all ears. I don't mean to hog the conversation."

"I like to listen to you talk." Immediately after the words had left her mouth, her face grew fiery, and she wished she could reel her idiotic utterance back in.

But Bill just kept on driving, hitting every bump and pothole, collecting each giggle from Fiona. Misty held on and collected them too. She'd never noticed before how much human laughter could sound like music. She would write down the observation in her newest journal, the most recent addition to her pile of fifty-odd volumes crammed with her wonderings. Music and laughter—how similar, how precious.

They reached Lawrence's trailer, and Misty's stomach tightened. There was no dog tied anywhere that she could see. Perhaps Lawrence had relented and come to his senses. He and Jellybean must be hunkered down and centering themselves, whatever that meant, and the film shoot would resume. She could find another dog trainer or maybe an out-of-work musician who could play the violin all day to keep Jellybean in check. Hope sprang anew in her heart.

She knocked on the door. "Mr. Tucker? I mean, Lawrence? It's Misty Agnelli. Are you and Jellybean okay?"

The inside of the trailer was still and quiet. They might be napping, but Jellybean could hear a potato chip drop at fifty paces, so he wouldn't sleep through Misty's assertive knocking.

Now her optimism began to waver, and worry took its place. She pulled the latch on the door and opened it a crack.

"Mr. Tucker?" she called into the gap.

Bill moved by her and pushed inside. "I'd better check."

She followed him, and Fiona climbed in behind them. The trailer was empty. No sign of the actor or his dog.

"Where is he?" Misty said aloud.

Bill picked up a piece of paper from the table and frowned. "I'm not sure, but I think you'd better read this. It's addressed to you."

∾

Bill watched as she snatched the paper and read it. Twice. "I know the words, but I don't get what he's trying to say."

"Read it aloud. Maybe I can pick up the gist."

"My dear Misty," she read. "My heart is heavy, burdened. How I admire you for being able to lose yourself in your music, to cast off your worries and sink yourself deep. I am disturbed of soul and spirit, and I must depart for a while to find my center, to"—she squinted at the handwriting—"reconnect myself with my essence." She quirked a brow at Bill.

"He's taking a break," he translated.

"All that to say he needs a vacation?"

"Actors."

She read the last part. "I will return when I have done so. I commit him into your tender care until my return." She stared at Bill. "What does he mean 'commit him into my tender care'?"

Like a perfectly cued line from a film, at that moment Larry nudged open the door with his foot. He sported an oven mitt on each hand, and clasped between them was a snarling Jellybean.

Larry held the dog as if he were an unexploded mortar. "He was tied to my door with a note that said I should watch him until you got here. Uh-uh. I don't get paid enough for that. Here."

He thrust the dog at Misty, and Jellybean set about happily licking her chin.

"But—" she started.

"Forget it." Larry slammed out the door. "I'm outta here."

Misty stared at the dog, who kept winding up in her arms in

spite of her best efforts. "How long does it take someone to reconnect with their essence?"

Bill searched for something helpful to offer. "Good question. I've never really known anyone to do that. Most people I know take a weekend trip and come back refreshed."

"But Lawrence Tucker is not most people."

"You're right about that."

She stared at the dog and sank into the kitchen chair. Jellybean continued his licking, his nose quivering at the sight of Fiona. "I just can't get rid of this creature." It came out as a whimper, and she bit her lip. "And I want to go home."

Bill settled into the chair opposite, his nosiness getting the better of him. "May I ask, if it's not too personal, why you're so miserable here? I mean, they're paying you to stay in a beach town on a movie set. Most people would jump at the chance."

"I guess I'm like Lawrence Tucker. Neither of us are like most people."

He sat quietly, studying her.

The quiet appeared to tease an admission out of her. "I don't like change. It…scares me. I want things to be normal and routine."

"Your grandmother said you, er, became a bit more tentative after your father's accident."

She blushed. "Yes, my natural reclusive tendencies went out of control when my father was hit by a car while he was walking the dog. They didn't think he would live." She expelled a slow breath. "We lived in a really small town outside San Bernardino, and this parade of people, literally dozens of them, would arrive every day at home or at the hospital, and I heard them whisper all the things the doctors said. Broken neck, possible infection, ruptured spleen. I wanted them all to leave." The words seemed to explode from her. "If they would just leave us alone, I knew Dad would get better."

Bill nodded, waiting for the rest.

"I sort of stopped wanting to be around people. I would hide under my dad's bed and refuse to go to school. If I could just stay with him and be quiet and keep the people away, I knew he would be okay."

"And he healed?"

"Yes. God brought my father back to us. He recovered almost completely, but…I guess I didn't. I never got over that feeling of wanting to stay under the bed and be invisible." Jellybean sniffed the knee of her jeans. "I stick to my regular routine and I'm okay."

"Does your routine include other people?" Again, a nosy question.

She started. "Of course. I see Nana regularly and my family. I have five siblings."

"When you see them, is it in person or on Skype?"

"Both," she mumbled. "I know what you're thinking. Lawrence gave me a talk about letting my light shine too, but I've learned I can shine my light just fine using Skype and writing notes to people, or by the occasional phone call."

"Those are good things, but rubbing elbows with people is pretty good too."

"God would not have made me so prone to social disaster if He wanted me to rub elbows."

Bill chuckled. "I've had my own share of public disasters, for sure. So…no boyfriend in your life? Whoops, sorry. Not my business."

"I dated a man while I was earning my master's in music. Jack was a part-time saxophonist and a business major. I used to go out more. With him. We went to museums and flea markets and coffee shops, and I got better at that rubbing elbows thing, but he's gone now."

He saw a flicker of pain cross her face.

"He loves someone else." Jellybean licked her cheeks, and she buried her face in his silky coat.

"Oh. I'm sorry. Believe me, I know how that feels."

"It's perfectly logical," Misty babbled. "His fiancée is extremely pretty, and she's a party planner. Her name is Jill, so it's funny—Jack and Jill. She's so confident. It's as if she owns the room wherever she goes. I've never felt that way."

"Yeah," he said quietly. "My girlfriend in high school was like that. She had a million-dollar smile that lit up my soul. We dated for three years, and I never could figure out why a girl like that went out with a guy like me."

"Why didn't you stay together?"

"I would have, but she found someone else too. Someone smarter." The word sounded harsh, and he wished he could take it back.

Misty looked puzzled. "But you're really smart, and everyone likes you."

"Smart? No. That's for people with schooling and degrees and such."

"People don't need degrees to be smart."

"How many?"

"What?"

"How many degrees do you have?"

She stroked Jellybean's wiry topknot. "Well, um, I have a BA and a master's in music theory."

"And?"

"Well, and…I've started on a PhD."

"But if you didn't have any of those things, would you still feel like you were smart?"

"I never really thought about it. My family is full of academic types. It was never a question about whether or not to get a degree, but rather which ones."

"My family is the academic type too, but I'm not." *Don't say another word, Bill, not another word.*

"Nana doesn't have a degree, and she's the smartest person I know."

Did she really believe that? Well-meaning people would often voice similar sentiments. *You're smart in a different way, Bill.* Just not in the way that allowed a fellow to succeed, that paved the way for a man to earn dignity and respect enough to hold his head up.

How could a man feel smart when he couldn't fill out a job application? When he had to order a hamburger at every restaurant he ever went to because he couldn't decipher the menu? How would Misty look at him if she knew? He glanced away and cleared his throat. "Anyway, if you really need to get back home, I'll take Jellybean for you."

She gaped. "You would do that?"

"Sure. He can hang out in the chocolate shop until Lawrence comes back."

Misty looked as though she'd won the lottery. She could go home. He shook off a touch of sadness.

"That would be really nice of you."

He shrugged. "It's okay. Come here, dog-o."

Misty gathered him up to hand over to Bill. Jellybean began to whine.

"Fine way to treat a guy," Bill said as he took the end of the leash.

Misty Agnelli looked as though the weight of the world had been lifted off her shoulders. She was free.

Eight

Bill wondered how soon he would regret his magnanimous gesture. Jellybean sensed a change in the air and tried to bolt, but Bill had managed to snag the leash before the dog escaped.

Fiona held up her hands, wanting to hold the leash.

"You can take charge of Jellybean, Fee, but let's wash first," Bill said, eyeing the red smears on her fingers. "You're all sticky from the lollipop. Go in the bathroom and clean up."

Fiona's mouth pinched into a stubborn pucker, and she shook her head.

"Go now, Fee," Bill said, "or you can't hold the leash."

Fiona refused. When she did not get the coveted leash, she sat hard on her bottom, stuck her fingers in her mouth, and began to smack her feet against the floor. Soon tears gushed down her face. Bill looked on in confusion.

"Uh…"

Fiona's shoes whomped harder, vibrating the linoleum. Jellybean would have thrown himself onto the pounding limbs if Bill hadn't held fast to the leash.

Fiona's face grew wet with tears, and her nose ran.

Bill felt panic building inside as he looked around for someone to come and handle the problem, until he realized he was now that someone. The choices spooled through his brain. Should he reason with her? Carry her to the bathroom and forcibly wash her hands? Give her the silly leash already to stop the eruption?

"I haven't seen her do this before," he said out of the corner of his mouth to Misty.

Misty cocked her head. "It's a temper tantrum. Pretty common for this age."

Common? He'd never seen her do it when Dillon and Bella were alive. It was the kind of thing he would call his mother about if he wasn't so worried that his father would answer the phone. Then it would be a tense chat in which he tried to paint the success of Chocolate Heaven in glowing colors and his father attempted to sound interested in his son's newest ridiculous venture. Nope. He'd have to figure this one out on his own.

Fiona kicked so hard one of her shoes flew off, sending Jellybean into a barking frenzy as he lunged for it until Bill pulled him back. Misty appeared completely calm.

"What should I do?" he asked.

"Nothing."

Nothing? "Huh? That doesn't seem right. She's really upset. I should be doing something."

"Doing nothing is doing something. You just let her have her blowup, and most importantly, you don't let her get her way until she does what you want."

He tried to keep the doubt from his voice. "Are you sure? She's been through a lot." His voice dropped to a whisper. "Losing her parents and moving here. It turned her world upside down." *Along with mine*, he thought. It was a nutty world indeed when Bill Woodson became the disciplinarian.

"That's true, but she needs to feel like you're a parent, and a parent says no sometimes. She needs walls to bounce off of so she knows she's safe."

The word *parent* startled Bill. It was the first moment it had actually dawned on him that he was now, for better or for worse, Fiona's parent. The notion started twin rivers of love and terror coursing through him. "I haven't really thought about it like that…I mean, that I'm her parent now. Not just Uncle Bill." He stared at Fiona a while longer. "This is a permanent job, isn't it?"

A note of something shone in Misty's face. Could it be admiration? He didn't see how.

"Yes, it is. You've taken on a lot."

He blew out a breath. "There was no other choice, really. My parents aren't in good health, and Fiona's aunt, Bella's sister, is a geophysicist for an oil company, so she's all over the world. She was in Africa at the tail end of a yearlong assignment when the accident happened."

"There is always another choice." She reached out and put a tentative hand on his forearm. "You stepped up. That took an amazing amount of courage."

Yes, it was admiration he saw in her coffee-colored eyes. He let himself savor the feel of her hand on his arm for a moment until doubts crept in. Dillon and Bella were smart achiever types, a far cry from a guy who was struggling to make a living selling sweets. His heart, not his head, had led him to take in his little niece. He would never measure up in the parenting department. There were just not enough YouTube videos to shape Bill Woodson into a sharp enough parent for Fiona. Worry bubbled up inside him.

His mother's words echoed in his heart. "God made you to shine a light, Bill. You don't get to pick what kind of candle you get." He figured he'd been allotted a tiny birthday candle compared to a petawatt laser he'd seen on TV. Still, he thought, straightening, if God gave him a puny birthday candle, he might as well make the flicker useful.

"Okay. So I do nothing," he murmured to bolster his courage. "Right."

Together they watched the tantrum build to storm levels, Jellybean barking his concern. Just when he was about at his breaking point, when he feared Fiona was about to asphyxiate in her rage, it was over. She sat up and looked at Bill. Bill looked at Misty. Misty gave him a reassuring nod. Jellybean shook his ears as if in encouragement.

Bill cleared his throat. "Go wash now, Fiona."

Fiona got up, put on her runaway shoe, and went to the trailer bathroom to wash her hands.

Bill tried not to gape outright at his first parenting success.

"You were right. It did work."

Misty laughed. "Yeah."

When Fiona returned, Bill handed her the leash, and Jellybean was delighted to lead her outside into the sunshine.

In a flood of excitement and gratitude, Bill gave in to his feelings and wrapped Misty in a hug.

"Thank you," he murmured, pressing his lips to the perfect shell of her ear.

His heart danced up to a faster tempo at the feel of her soft body, the press of her silken hair against his cheek. He imagined she relaxed in his embrace, leaned her head to his chest, welcomed their sudden connection.

When he released her, his senses were dizzied.

She blinked, cheeks pink. "You're welcome," she said. "Anytime. You can, um, Skype me or maybe even call if you come across anything else."

He'd made her uncomfortable. He sighed. "Where did you learn how to handle a tantrum? Child psychology classes?"

"Nope. Having five siblings."

"Can't learn stuff like that in a classroom, huh?"

"I had to rub elbows, so to speak."

He laughed and she joined in.

Misty was still feeling off balance as they returned to Chocolate Heaven. Bill, Fiona, and Jellybean rode in the golf cart, and this time Misty followed in her grumbly VW. She'd wanted to make a clean break of it, but Wilson was having a staff meeting in his trailer, and she dared not disturb him to tell him of her imminent departure, so she resolved to return after she collected Nana Bett. It was the upheaval that left her feeling nonplussed, she told herself, not the lingering feeling of Bill's embrace.

He was grateful, that was all, and she was out of practice with the hugging of men. Bill was an amazing man, a patient, helpful soul to take on the rascally Jellybean, and she resolved to send him a very graciously worded thank-you note for his dog assistance and a heartfelt apology that she might have inadvertently put the kibosh on his grand opening. Maybe she should send along a little something. A plant? A fruit basket? A subscription to a doggy-treat-of-the-month club?

She sighed. Knowing Jellybean, a doggy straitjacket might be more useful.

Nana Bett still stood watch in the empty store. She beamed, gesturing to the empty top shelf of the glass cabinet.

Bill tied an outraged Jellybean to the lamppost outside the store and hurried in. "What happened? Were we robbed?"

"No," Nana said. "A certain wonderful customer came in and bought the whole batch—violins, jelly jumbles, and all."

"Who?" Misty asked, incredulous.

"You'll never guess."

Gunther came in from the back. "That wackadoodle actor."

Misty tried to decipher the mystery. "You mean…"

Nana Bett nodded. "The great Lawrence Tucker himself."

"When? Where did he go? Why?" Misty sputtered, running to the window to peer out.

"He left in a taxi about a half hour ago."

She sagged. "Did he say where he was headed?"

Nana clucked her tongue. "He's had a hard time. The acting business is a meat grinder, especially if you're not a spring chicken anymore."

"But he walked away from all those people who are depending on him. He just…turned his back on them."

Nana pursed her lips. "Sometimes that's the only way a person can cope."

Misty remembered those days when she'd hidden under her father's bed, praying that no one would find her. Her heart lurched until she reminded herself she'd been a child then, a little girl. *But aren't you doing the same thing now?* her conscience prodded. *A tiny apartment from which you hardly ever emerge? A life lived through Skype?* She zipped up her jacket and refocused. *This isn't about me. It's about Lawrence.*

"I'm going to tell the director that I'm leaving."

"Isn't there another way?" Nana asked, a dangerous plea in her voice.

"No," Misty said firmly. "There isn't. Come with me back to the set, and then I'll drive you home."

"But what about the festival?"

"What festival?"

Bill shrugged. "We were planning a six-week festival for the duration of the shoot. Just special sales and weekend activities for the tourists. The history museum was going to put up a WWII display and stuff like that. I guess that's all off if the film is belly-up."

"Isn't there something you can do, honey?" Nana Bett beamed her laser gaze on Misty.

A ribbon of discomfort snaked through her belly at the thought of Bill and all the others and the end of their festival plans. But what could she do? Lawrence was gone. She was not the man's keeper, or his dog's.

"There really isn't," she told Nana. "I'm sorry, Bill. Very sorry."

Their eyes met, and though she saw disappointment in his spring-grass eyes, they held no blame. Bill was too good a man for that. If things were different, if she was different, one of those self-assured, charming women, like the one from Bill's high school, she might have hugged him, gathered close the muscular frame of that man who had taken on the mantle of parenthood in spite of his fear. She would have relished the connection that she'd experienced in the trailer, the sweet sensation of being close to another, cherished the proximity, basked in the easy affection.

Instead, she gave him an awkward wave as she guided her grandmother out of the shop and back to her car. "Thanks for everything, Bill." She patted Jellybean on the head as she went by. He plopped his fuzzy bottom on the sidewalk, and she thought the look he gave her was full of reproach.

Nana wasn't about to let the chance to meet a real live movie director sail by, so she accompanied Misty to Mr. Wilson's trailer, where he was lying on his back with a damp washcloth over his eyes.

"Who is it?" he said. "I've already given my pound of flesh, so unless you're bringing coffee or my missing actor, go away."

"Er, it's Misty Agnelli."

"Who?"

"The violin tutor."

"And her grandma," Nana put in.

Mr. Wilson didn't answer, but his gusty sigh briefly inflated the washcloth.

"I just wanted to tell you I'm leaving. Bill Woodson, a shop owner in town, the one who makes those chocolates…you know, the ones with the little sprinkle things on top?"

"Uh-huh."

"Well, he's got Jellybean. He agreed to take care of him until Mr. Tucker comes back."

Mr. Wilson bolted to a sitting position, the washcloth splatting to the floor. "I don't give a rat's patootie what happens to that dog. I'm shooting all the scenes we can until Friday, and if Lawrence Tucker isn't back by then, my producers are pulling the plug, and that dog can stay with the candy man for all I care."

"Pulling the plug?" Misty queried.

Nana nodded. "That means they won't make the movie, not now. Say, since you're up, Mr. Wilson," she said, offering up her blue autograph book, "would you mind giving me your autograph?"

He blinked, grabbed the book, and signed it as if it were one of the zillions of papers his assistant handed him each day. "If Tucker doesn't return by Friday, this movie won't ever see the light of day," Wilson snapped.

"Maybe you could get another actor?" Misty suggested. "One without a dog?"

Wilson huffed. "Let's face it, this isn't exactly a blockbuster production in the first place. Tucker is past his prime, and he was lucky to get this gig, but if he doesn't haul himself back to the set by Friday, there will be no movie. And once word gets out that he abandoned ship, Tucker won't have a career either."

"Mr. Tucker," Nana corrected.

"Yeah, well, he'll be a has-been, because no one will sign him once they hear how he bugged out on this film. He'll be lucky to get work on denture commercials."

"That's terrible," Misty said.

Wilson lifted a shoulder. "That's business."

"So all the actors and film crew…they'll be out of work too?"

"We'll land on our feet. We can go back to Los Angeles and find other gigs."

And when that happened there would be no more festival, no

more tour buses, and likely no more career for Lawrence Tucker. Her stomach tightened down to walnut size.

This is not your problem, she reassured herself. *There is nothing you can do about it.* "Okay, well, thanks very much, Mr. Wilson."

He nodded absently. "Hey, can you tell that Bill guy to bring us some more of those sprinkle candies?" He waved a hand. "Ah, never mind. You're leaving. I'll have my assistant phone him."

On the way to the car, Nana looked for Larry, the unfortunate Jellybean wrangler. "I want his autograph too. He was hilarious trying to get that dog out of the tank. I think he could have a future in physical comedy."

But Larry must have been elsewhere, so Misty started the car slowly along the narrow road that led out of Albatross, her mind churning along with the wheels.

No Tucker.

No movie.

No help for Bill.

Nana was uncharacteristically quiet.

"There's nothing I could have done," Misty blurted out.

Nana nodded.

"I mean, I don't even know where Mr. Tucker is."

"That's true."

"And even if I did, it's not my job to talk to him. These people, these actors, are from a different world. I'm just a musician. I can't talk anybody into anything. I'm not good with people in the first place, let alone movie people."

More nodding.

They were approaching the one and only stop sign at the end of Main Street. Then Albatross would be behind them. Permanently. It would become an odd adventure to add to her journal. Really, the only adventure she'd recorded in a very long while. But what a sad ending for Lawrence, for Jellybean.

For Bill.

"It's not my responsibility," she repeated firmly, allowing the words to stoke her courage. "There is no reason for me to stay here."

"Just one thing," Nana said, peering into the side-view mirror as they rolled away from the stop sign.

"What?"

"The dog doesn't seem to care about your reasons."

"What dog?"

Nana pointed out her window at Jellybean as he jogged along the side of the road, trailing a section of chewed leash, keeping pace with the car. "That one."

Nine

Bill sat in a bleary haze in front of the computer screen the next morning, staring at the keyboard and the photo of Jellybean he was trying to make into a missing-dog poster.

He'd realized the dog/beaver had chewed through the leash shortly after Misty and Nana Bett departed. All day Friday he'd combed the town, searching every hole and crevice in Albatross while Gunther minded the store, which was painfully empty of customers. He had no idea how to contact Misty and tell her he'd lost the critter, and he wasn't sure she'd want to know anyway. It was clear she wanted nothing more to do with the dog, the movie people, or the town of Albatross.

Or him.

Why did that thought sting? She was a casual acquaintance, a woman who liked her own quiet world, and she'd flat out said as much. Nothing personal against him. Probably just the pride of a likable man who wasn't as likable as he thought. *Thanks for the humility, God.*

Seemed like he was learning plenty of other lessons in humility at the moment. Misty and his ego aside, he was worried about that nutty terrier running lose, getting into who knew what kind of trouble. He chugged some coffee, put thoughts of the caramel-eyed Misty Agnelli out of his mind, and tried to focus again.

He pushed the Print button and produced the picture he'd found after typing "Lawrence Tucker's dog" into the search box. That had taken some time even with the computer's intuitive spelling help.

The picture came out, the animal appearing vastly more angelic and adorable than the stinker had a right to, and Bill found an old marker in the desk drawer. He laboriously wrote across the top: MISSING DOG. CONTACT BILL. Then he added his phone number and email address.

He was twiddling with the pen when he realized it was nearly nine. A special emergency meeting of the Silver Screen Festival organizers had been called, and he'd offered the shop as a meeting place. He had a feeling it would be a short gathering. No Lawrence Tucker. No movie. No festival. Meeting adjourned.

He found Fiona looking at books in her bed and hustled her into a set of almost matching, nearly clean clothes. She tugged on his pant leg and pointed to the backyard.

"No, honey. Jellybean is still missing."

Her brow furrowed dangerously, and her lower lip turned down in a disappointed curve.

"Maybe he went over to play with Lunk. We'll ask Gunther when he comes in, okay?"

When she was munching toast with strawberry jelly—not the dreaded preserves she detested, as he'd finally managed to discern—he hurried to make coffee, putting out as many of the leftover chocolates from the day before as he could.

Vivian Buckley was the first to arrive, with Tinka tucked under her arm. She declined a seat and the coffee he offered.

"I heard that the shoot is off."

"Where did you hear that?"

"Larry told me Lawrence did a cut and run. They can't do the movie without him, can they?"

Bill had no idea what they could or couldn't do. "I don't know, but maybe we should wait for official word from the director."

"The woman left. That violin teacher."

He nodded. "Yes. She went home."

Roger Tillson came next, a skinny man with a bald spot on the top of his head at odds with the long ponytail down his back. He was the proprietor of Albatross Hardware and the president of the historical society. "I'm all set with the presentation for next weekend. Got volunteers dressing up in WWII uniforms, and we're setting up a miniature display of the Battle of Guadalcanal. It's gonna be epic."

Vivian regarded him coldly. "I tried to tell you this morning that Lawrence up and left. They're not going to film the movie. The whole thing is most likely off."

Roger helped himself to coffee. "Ah, I heard that was just a tiff. Actors are all uppity and such, not like normal people. They'll get it straightened out."

"I hope so." Volunteer fire chief Toby Gillespie was next into the shop, beelining immediately for a napkin, which he heaped with chocolates. His plaid shirt did not quite restrain his stomach from peeking through the gaps between the buttons. "We got the fire engine all shined up, and we're ready to give tours of the station."

"How does that fit in with a movie festival theme anyway?" Vivian asked.

"It doesn't, but kids like to climb on fire engines, and these movie lovers are gonna have kids with them, aren't they? That's why you're allowing kids at your Movie Time Tea Party or whatever it is that you're hosting at the Lady Bird."

Vivian rolled her eyes. "I might as well cancel the order with the florist and the party rental place. I'm not going to need all those round tables after all."

Roger did not appear to have heard. "Oh yeah. People will lug their kids along too. We've got a genuine tank on loan from the Half Moon Bay Historical Society, and the young'uns are going to be all over that. You know, I was thinking—we could do this every year, even after the film has wrapped. It could be our shtick, you know? Every town needs a shtick. Half Moon Bay has the Pumpkin Festival, and Gilroy has the Garlic Festival. We need one too."

"If you'd stop being so Pollyanna for one minute," Vivian snapped, "you'd realize that there isn't going to be a movie filmed in Albatross. It's all over, thanks to Lawrence. The festival has ended before it ever began."

Roger licked a smear of chocolate off his finger. "That's just a rumor. Tucker is probably resting or something, or it's a publicity stunt. I read about that kind of thing all the time on Facebook."

"No, it's not a rumor. I've known him since he was seventeen." Her voice was strained and tight. "Lawrence is an emotional coward."

An emotional coward? That was a new one to Bill.

"He's coming back," Toby said complacently. "You'll see."

"Okay, I'll bite," Vivian said. "How exactly do you know that, Toby? You've never even met him."

Toby unfurled a napkin and wiped his face with a flourish. "Because he left his dog, didn't he? That means he's coming back. A man doesn't just leave his dog."

Vivian huffed out an enormous breath that ruffled Tinka's fur and aimed a look at Bill. "Do you want to explain it to them?"

"Well…" Bill started.

"Well what?" Toby said, reaching for another chocolate. "I heard you're watching Tucker's dog, right? So he'll be back."

Bill felt the weight of three pairs of eyes on him. The flicker in his stomach made him realize how Misty must feel when she was suddenly the center of attention.

"Here's what I know about the situation," he said. "Yes, Lawrence left town, and yes, he left his dog behind."

"But he's coming back, in your opinion?" Roger said. "Right?"

He wanted to say yes, but rather than lie, he stayed silent.

Vivian sighed. "He dumped the dog on you, didn't he? Or the violin tutor did."

"No, not *dumped*," he replied. "I offered to take charge of him."

"So you're watching Jellybean?" Vivian asked.

"Yes. And no."

Vivian stroked Tinka and skewered him with a look. "How can it be yes and no?"

"I was watching the dog, but…"

"But what?"

But the dog ran away and Misty is gone, so now there is absolutely no reason why Lawrence would return to Albatross. He sucked in a breath.

Suddenly a scrambling of claws could be heard on the cement outside. And then, to his utter astonishment, Misty stepped into the shop, clutching Jellybean. The dog perked up when he spotted Tinka and barked out a high-pitched greeting.

Bill's spirit leaped at the sight of Misty standing there, her strong musician's fingers holding tight to the squirming dog.

"See?" Roger said in triumph. "Jellybean is still in town, and that means Lawrence Tucker is not far behind."

"Well…hi," Bill managed.

Misty wiggled her only free finger. "Am I…interrupting a meeting?"

"Just planning out the Silver Screen Festival," Roger said. "Gonna be epic. So everything's a go then?"

Misty looked uncertain. "What?"

"I mean, we can set things in motion for next weekend, right? 'Cuz Tucker is coming back, and the movie is going to be shot here after all." Roger's smile showed all his crooked front teeth.

Misty looked from Bill to Vivian to the staring men. Then she cleared her throat, and her answer came out as a squeak. "Yes."

Roger and Toby high-fived each other and left the shop, exchanging details about tanks and howitzers. The door closed behind them, leaving Vivian still staring and Misty still preventing Jellybean's dash to his lady love.

"So," Vivian said, holding Tinka closer, "you're back, Misty."

She nodded.

"And you really believe Lawrence will return?"

She nodded again.

Vivian was thoughtful for a moment. Bill could see the gleam of disbelief tangled with a hopeful yearning. Part of Vivian wanted to be proven right about Lawrence—that he was a selfish, weak disappointment—and part of her desperately wanted to be wrong.

She caught Bill looking at her and gave her head a little toss. "I hope you're right. There's a lot at stake for Albatross."

Bill noticed Misty's throat move as she swallowed—hard.

"He'll be back," Misty mumbled.

Vivian gathered Tinka and left.

Bill didn't know why his body was so tense, but he blew out a breath.

"Misty," he said in his best Ricky Ricardo imitation, "you've got some 'splaining to do."

"It's complicated."

He ushered her out into the backyard, where she released Jellybean to play with a delighted Fiona.

"I'm all ears."

Misty accepted the cup of coffee Bill handed her, and though she was too timid to ask, he somehow intuited that now was precisely the right moment for chocolate. He placed his own coffee and the chocolates on a small patio table, and they settled into the slightly rusted chairs.

"Two salted caramels. That should at least get us through the part where you explain how in the world you have come into possession of Jellybean Tucker again," Bill said.

She didn't answer at first, overwhelmed at the glory of that gooey chocolate wonder settling across her taste buds and the sweet sensation of being near Bill once again. Both were heady pleasures. He waited patiently.

"If you can believe it, he was following my car out of town. We scooped him up, and I drove Nana home to Berkeley and stayed the night at her place, though Jellybean was extremely unkind to Nana's canary, Peepers. It's the only time I've known Peepers to go silent. Usually, he can't be quieted for anything. I called and left a message on your shop phone. Didn't you get it?"

He groaned. "I didn't think to look. I've been out hitting the bricks, hunting for Jellybean."

At the sound of his name, the dog raced up to Bill, placed one tiny paw on his leg, and licked a spot on his jeans. When Bill reached out to pet him, he burst away and commenced running frantic laps around the yard, much to Fiona's amusement.

"Okay, that explains the return of Wonder Dog." Bill directed those intense green eyes in her direction, and she felt a tingle that started in her stomach and ran through her body like a swiftly played scale.

"But why did you tell them Lawrence would come back? Did you hear from him?"

"No."

"Did the director say the movie is going forward anyway?"

"No. He's pulling the plug Friday if Lawrence doesn't return."

Bill's eyebrows rose halfway to his thick hair. "I give. Why did you come back, Misty?"

Why? Why? The very question, the heart of the matter. Why had Misty Agnelli returned to Albatross when she'd nearly made her escape, hidden safely under the bed again while the world went crazy around her? "These are good chocolates," she said, stuffing the second one into her mouth.

"Candy will not save you, young lady." He leaned forward. "Why, Misty?"

The caramel bought her a few precious moments. She swallowed and forced her mouth to say the words. "I'm going to find Lawrence Tucker and bring him back here before Wilson stops the production." There. It was delivered, sitting like an unexploded bomb between them.

Bill froze. "You think you can do that? Get him to return?"

"Yes," she blurted before she could rethink it.

"How? Did you call him?"

"No."

He scrubbed a hand across his unshaven jaw. "Did he contact you?"

"No."

"Then how are you going to find him? He could be anywhere."

"I'm going to…" She stopped. "I don't know."

Bill shook his head. "But why would you do that, Misty?"

Why indeed? "I can't explain it. It won't make sense." It didn't make one bit of sense, even in her own mind. Borderline recluse, walking social disaster, coward to the nth degree.

"Doesn't have to make sense. Tell me."

She wanted time to compose the right words, to neatly score them to the proper rhythm, in an appropriate time signature. Bill's piercing gaze would not allow her the luxury.

She sucked in a deep breath, wishing she had more chocolate. "I felt like I was meant to come back here and convince Lawrence to return."

He stared.

"For the town," she added. *And for you.* At least she had the sense not to tell that bit.

Now he was openly gaping. "You were meant to find Tucker?"

"Somebody has to do it."

His open mouth gave way to the quirk of a smile.

"And for some crazy reason, I think God figures that's supposed to be me," she finished.

"Let it shine, Misty," she could hear Lawrence saying. Okay. She'd just set the match to the wick, and there was no turning back. Stomach knotted, she waited for his response.

"So a woman who is scared to leave home has returned to a town she doesn't like to find a man she doesn't understand without any idea how to go about it, on a one-week deadline?"

The knot grew tighter. He would laugh. Think her crazy. Wish her well and step away from the strange, awkward, ridiculous woman who was Misty Agnelli.

He did laugh, and her mortification was complete. The rich, sonorous bass filled the tiny backyard. She stood, fiddling with her empty coffee cup, cheeks hot with embarrassment, hands cold with shame. What had she expected?

"Well, anyway," she said, "I'll take Jellybean and get out of your hair."

He wiped a hand across his eyes. "I just can't believe this."

"Thanks for keeping him, or at least trying to." She was two steps away when he caught her by the arm.

"Wait a minute."

She would not turn and see the mirth on his face, the humor she'd provided at the cost of her own dignity. "I'm in a hurry," she muttered. "Mr. Wilson said I could stay in the trailer, so I'll take Jellybean there."

But he did not let go. He gently turned her around until she was looking into the handsome face, at the strong chin and slightly untidy hair.

"You don't think God meant for you to do this alone, do you?"

She blinked hard to dismiss the tears that had gathered in her eyes when she'd heard him laughing. "What do you mean?"

"I mean, Misty Agnelli," he said, beaming a smile at her that left her positively breathless, "you've got yourself a partner in this quest."

Was she imagining this? Dreaming it up like some romantic movie? Had Bill Woodson really believed her wacky notion enough to help? Enough to stay close? To her? A partner.

Jellybean barked and chased his tail as Fiona looked on with glee.

"Correct that. Looks like you've got yourself three partners. Can you deal with that?"

She nodded, not trusting her voice. Suddenly, she did not feel quite so awkward and unsure of herself as she had a moment before.

Partners. Yes, she could deal with that.

Ten

Bill figured he was going to be a poor excuse for a detective, but for some reason he was thrilled just to sit with Misty in Lawrence's unoccupied trailer, trying to narrow down the endless scenarios to explain where the actor had gone. The director had allowed the amateur detectives to search for clues in the star's domicile and even provided Tucker's cell phone number.

"Do whatever you want," he said. "I've got other things to take care of. Oh, and thanks for the chocolates," Wilson said, looking at Bill as if he were a celebrity. "How do you get that combination of creamy and crunch in those peanut butter puffy things?"

"Trade secret," Bill joked.

Wilson nodded soberly. "I understand. I worked on a film where everyone had to sign secrecy agreements."

"Which one was that?" Misty asked.

"I can't tell you."

After Wilson left, Misty eagerly dialed Tucker's cell phone number and received no response. There wasn't much in the trailer that was any more helpful. Tucker, it seemed, loved to read fishing magazines and consume vast quantities of green olives and tiny gherkin pickles, both of which were well represented in the minuscule refrigerator.

After a lunch of peanut butter sandwiches and apple slices, they decided to track down the taxi driver who, Bill had ascertained from Vivian, must have been dispatched from the cab company in nearby Tidewater. They set off, Bill driving his growling delivery van, which smelled of chocolate, with Fiona in the backseat and Misty riding shotgun.

It was a glorious spring morning, and Bill cracked the window to let in the sea air. "Do you mind if I pop in some tunes?"

She laughed when he loaded up the *Farm Fandango* CD, which was Fiona's current favorite, and soon they were both singing along to nursery school songs.

He saw Misty's fingers tapping a complicated pattern on her knee.

"You're fingering the music in your mind, aren't you?"

She nodded. "You got me. Can't help myself."

What would it be like to be so gifted? "That's incredible."

"What?"

"To be so good at something that it's in your blood and nerves and muscles."

"Like you and chocolate."

He chuckled. "I don't have chocolate in my blood, I hope. That would be killer on the cholesterol."

She giggled, and he heard another sound from the backseat, the soft burble of humming from Fiona. His hushed awe must have translated, because Misty stopped singing to listen.

And then it stopped as quickly as it had started.

He did not realize there were tears in his eyes until one trickled down his cheek. He hastened to rub it away. "Sorry," he whispered. "It's one of the first sounds I've heard her make since…" He swallowed hard.

Misty reached for his hand and squeezed. "Better than music."

He held on to her fingers and marveled at how he'd gotten to be in this driver's seat, relishing a child's hum, chasing after a missing star, enjoying the company of a musician. How exactly had he gotten acquainted with a bona fide musical genius?

Because she doesn't know, said the darkness inside him before he could stop it.

And she doesn't have to, he returned, sitting up straighter and clasping her hand more firmly.

Together they drove along the wind-scoured coast, listening to barnyard boogies and straining for any further sound from the backseat. As the CD finished up, they'd made it to Stan Fan's Taxi Company. Not daring to leave the sleepy Jellybean unattended, Bill held the dog, football style, and guided them all into the office.

Bill expected to find an old, balding guy smoking a stogie, but the man in charge was no more than midtwenties, he guessed, with a Bluetooth headset in his ear.

"Welcome to Stan Fan's Taxi Company," said the young man. His black eyes regarded them curiously from under a mop of hair. "I'm Stan. What can I do for you? Looking to hire a cab? Did you try to call? Sorry if I didn't pick up, but my dispatcher had to go have an emergency root canal, so I'm trying to keep us afloat until the novocaine wears off." He noticed Jellybean. "Hey, that's a cute dog." He extended a hand to pet Jellybean, but Bill casually shifted the dog to the other arm.

"He's, uh, missing his owner right now. Sort of down in the dumps."

"Aww. That's terrible. My dog Percy went missing when I was a kid. Never did find him. Broke my heart."

Misty explained their mission. "You picked up his owner, Lawrence Tucker, in Albatross on Friday. I need to know where he went."

"I remember the guy. He had a funny way of talking. All big and grand like, as if he was announcing the World Series or something."

Misty's face brightened. "Yes, that's him. We need to know his destination."

Stan's expression clouded. "Oh, um, that kind of thing is private. I don't disclose personal business about my clients. That's a no-no in the cab business unless there's been a murder or something like that." He raised a doubtful eyebrow. "You're not cops, are you?"

"No, but Mr. Tucker is a movie star, and he's gone missing. He's our friend, and he needs help."

"A movie star?" Stan blinked. "That could explain the weirdness, but he didn't look like anyone I know. What's he appeared in?"

Misty rattled off the names of a half dozen movies.

Stan remained blank. "Did he do any superhero movies?"

"I don't think so," Bill said.

"Oh, wait," Stan said, brightening. "Did they use his voice on the Galaxy Seven video game? I thought he sounded kinda familiar."

"Probably not," Bill said.

Getting back to their mission, Misty said, "It's really important that we find him."

Stan nodded. "Well, like I said, I can't help you with that."

Bill cautiously cuddled Jellybean closer. For once, the dog actually remained docile. Maybe he really did miss Tucker. Bill stroked the silky ears, and the dog relaxed under the attention, giving him a seriously pitiful look.

Bill let out a sigh, hoping it wasn't too dramatic. "Jellybean's had a rough time since Mr. Tucker left. He's escaped and run away from my place. I sure would like to reunite them."

"Yes," Misty hurried to put in. "Mr. Tucker saved Jellybean from drowning in a frozen lake. They've been inseparable ever since."

"Oh, wow. Dog probably wonders where his owner is."

Misty and Bill nodded in unison.

Stan's eyes went soft. "That must be heartbreaking. Poor little thing does look really down in the mouth. I always hoped that one day Percy would come barreling through the door again with that goofy bark of his. What I would have given for that to have happened. I never saw him again."

Misty was nodding so hard now her hair bounced around her face. "For sure, and we are so eager to reunite them, you wouldn't believe it."

Stan thought for a moment and then clicked at a laptop on the counter. "Tell you what. I won't give you the address, but I can tell you the city where I dropped him, okay?"

Bill and Misty exchanged a smile. Maybe they weren't such bad detectives after all.

Stan was grabbing for a pen when he suddenly spoke into his Bluetooth and disconnected. "Sorry. Family of four needs a ride to the airport pronto. They promised a nice tip if I'm there to pick them up in fifteen minutes."

"But we need that address," Bill said. "It's crucial."

Stan grabbed his keys off a hook on the wall. "Leave your number. I'll call you when I get back."

"We're on a deadline," Misty called as he ran past.

"Sorry, but I got college loans to pay off. I'll call you when I can."

Misty didn't put her cell phone down until they arrived back at Chocolate Heaven. Stan had not called. How long did it take to deliver a family to the airport anyway?

A timer on her phone pinged. "Oh, shoot. I've got a lesson to teach. Do you have an empty corner I can pop into? My violin's in my car, and if go back to the trailer, I'll be late."

"We'll get you set up. No problem."

After she grabbed her instrument from the trunk, Bill guided her upstairs. "You can use my room. It's not much bigger than a closet, but at least it isn't filled with brooms and dustpans."

Firing up her laptop, Misty got settled just in time for her noon lesson.

Ernest Finn's wrinkled face appeared on the screen. "Afternoon, Ms. Agnelli."

"Misty," she corrected him for the thousandth time. "How are you and the doggies?"

He chuckled. "Getting too old to chase after cats."

"You could consider a terrier. As far as I can tell, they don't ever get tired."

He laughed. "I'll stick with these mutts."

"Ready to get started?"

"Actually," he said, his puffy white brows wriggling on his forehead, "I'm afraid I've got to skip our lesson today."

"Oh?" She felt a stab of alarm. Ernest, a retired shopkeeper and a widower, had never missed his weekly lesson in the six years she'd been his teacher. He felt like family to Misty, right down to his grumpy old dogs and the six grandkids he'd shown her pictures of.

He knew a lot about Misty too, more about what was missing in her life than anything else. No boyfriend. No kids. No social life. Once she'd broken down and cried in between scales, actually sobbed out the ludicrous story of Jack and Jill. Ernest was a good listener, the best kind of friend, even if she'd never laid eyes on him in person. For just a moment, she had a deep longing to sit down face-to-face with Ernest.

"Is everything okay? Are you sick?" she pressed.

"Oh no, I'm fine. Just something came up. How is the film shooting going?"

"We've, uh… Well, it's sort of… Actually, it's hard to explain."

He frowned. "Still working there, right? Going to keep tutoring old Tuck on his violin, aren't you?"

More like keep chasing after him. "It's a little complicated."

He chewed his lip. "Well, don't give up on him, Misty. Could be he needs more than just a violin teacher."

That was an understatement. They made an appointment to reschedule the lesson and signed off. While Misty waited for Bruno, her teenage client in El Paso, to check in for his lesson, she scanned Bill's tidy room.

The bed was neatly made, and the tiny side table was bare of anything except an old cassette player and a brass alarm clock. The desk at which she sat barely fit into the corner, the wooden top scratched and dinged as if he'd owned it since childhood or bought it used. A small, faded photo was tacked to one corner of the desk. It was Bill in his high school football jersey, posed with the ball in one hand, one foot resting on a helmet that sat on the grass. He had a smile plastered on his face, but it looked forced rather than the genuine grin that tickled her insides every time she thought of it. The photo had been skewered with a tack that stuck right through the top of Bill's head, the pin jabbed so deeply into the wood that it made a crater in the photo.

She stared at it for a long time. There was something very sad about the tattered photo that she could not put her finger on. Why did she not see the self-assured confidence of a teen? The invincible spirit of a high school jock with the world lying at his feet, ready to conquer anything?

What would her own high school photo have shown? A girl hiding behind mounds of frizzy hair, books clutched to her baggy sweatshirt as if she could shield herself from life with academia. She would be alone in her picture also, no boyfriend by her side and, more painfully, no real girlfriends either. Her books and her music, those were her friends, her comforts in a home that she grew increasingly reluctant to leave. Maybe football was Bill's friend, though she didn't see how such a handsome, outgoing boy would have any trouble with his social life. He'd even had a beautiful girl-friend, so what could be lacking in his high school experience?

The only other thing on the desk was a manila envelope with papers jammed in untidily, protruding from the opening. Alphabet worksheets—Fiona's, no doubt. On the front of the envelope was a hand-drawn smiley face in girlish purple ink along with Bill's name and a heart before the other name. Dina.

The preschool teacher, of course. Just some extra practice for Fiona, who had no doubt missed quite a bit of her schooling when her parents were killed. Misty could picture the blond, petite Dina Everly, so lovely and at ease, from what Misty had seen when they picked up Fiona.

And the purple heart drawn before her name.

What did it mean, that heart from Dina to Bill?

And why did it matter?

It doesn't, Misty told herself firmly. *Bill is partnering with you only to find Lawrence because he has a vested interest in keeping the film shoot going.*

They were working together through the middle of the song to reach the finale.

Partners.

No more than that.

Turning back to the computer screen, she picked up her violin, soothed again by the smooth wood and coarse strings. She let her bow find a comforting tune to play as she waited for another student whom she had never actually met.

Eleven

The maddening Stan still had not called when Misty concluded her lessons at two o'clock.

When she reached for her cell phone to call him, Bill stopped her. "You've already left two messages. No sense hounding him, or he might change his mind about helping," he said with irritating practicality.

Gunther arrived with Lunk in tow.

"Can't leave him on account of he has taken to getting out. He's been better until recently." Gunther shot a look out the back window at Jellybean. "I blame that movie star dog. He's a bad influence. Like a canine gangster or something."

"But he's not a bad actor," Bill said. "You should have seen him earlier at the taxicab office. Completely pathetic." They all watched Jellybean bounding in graceful hops across the yard in pursuit of a grasshopper.

Gunther let Lunk out. The dog waddled to the grass and immediately flopped in a patch of sunshine. Lunk remained immovable in the face of Jellybean's relentless efforts to get him to play.

Gunther tied on his apron and surveyed the chocolate offerings. "You ain't sold anything since I been here?"

"Well, we had to close the shop to go to Tidewater."

"Might as well. Nobody in this town anyway 'cept for the residents."

Bill shook his head. "We're going to turn it all around next weekend when the Silver Screen Festival kicks off."

Gunther flapped a hand as if he were shooing away flies. "Whatever you say, boss. I'm getting paid whether we sell anything or not."

"That's the spirit," Bill said before turning to Misty. "I'm going to take Fiona to the park. Do you and Wonder Dog want come along?"

"But Stan might call."

"You've got your cell phone. He might just as well call us there as here. I'll pack peanut butter sandwiches."

"I thought you only knew how to make chocolate," she teased.

He grinned. "Very funny for someone who doesn't like small talk."

And it was, she was surprised to note. That was a humorous little phrase, right out of her very own mouth. Why did things feel easier when Bill was around? Even with Jack it had taken months to feel comfortable, like she didn't have to weigh each comment for potential awkwardness, measure each response against the yardstick of social norms, peer at other women to see what she should be wearing, saying, eating. But Bill made it easy, or perhaps she allowed herself to relax around him. She tucked the thought away to ponder it later.

He fixed the sandwiches and grabbed a juice box for Fiona, and they set off, Fiona holding Jellybean's new leash, the dog cheerfully dragging her in all directions as he sniffed every bush and plant on the way.

"It's so quiet here," Misty marveled as they traversed Main

Street. Her upstairs San Francisco apartment was situated above a bustling intersection, so there was a constant cacophony of noise from delivery trucks, construction workers, and bicycle messengers weaving in and out of it all.

"Like it?"

The quiet? Did she? "I've always loved the city because of the activity. No one pays any attention to anyone else."

"And that's a good thing?"

It had always seemed to her that it was—hiding in plain sight. But now that she had that "shine your light" thing going on in her heart, she wasn't sure anymore. She'd talked to more people in her short time in Albatross than she had in a year in San Francisco. The change was frightening, exhilarating, confusing. But not permanent, of course. The city and her apartment were waiting to receive her as soon as she managed to find Lawrence. She realized Bill was watching, head cocked, waiting for an answer.

"I'm not sure. The quiet is nice, for a while."

Bill helped Fiona onto a swing, and Misty pushed her from behind.

Bill was thoughtful. "That's kind of why I liked the ranch, in a way. Not having to schmooze or meet people's expectations."

"I would have thought you craved being around people. You're so outgoing."

He shrugged. "A defense mechanism. A good defense leads to a good offense."

"Defense against what?" She thought of the picture with the tack rammed into it. What was that hint of shame that appeared and disappeared like a swiftly played note?

He shrugged. "Not important. Doesn't matter anyway because I guess God wants me to be around people. He sure keeps drawing me into situations I never expected."

"Like fatherhood?"

"For sure." He pushed Fiona. "Okay, Fee. Time to learn to pump. You have to bend your legs on the upswing." He tried to demonstrate, looking so ridiculous with his long legs bent at odd angles that Misty laughed out loud.

She got onto the swing next to Fiona and held on to the chains, leaning way back with her feet up. "Like this. Up…"

Fiona mimicked her, and Bill scooted around to give them both a push from behind.

"Now down!" Misty hollered, pantomiming for the child.

Fiona bicycled her legs up and down. Swing by feeble swing, she finally got the motion mastered, and soon she was zooming up into the sky under her own momentum. Misty swung too, thrilled by their victory. To her great delight, Bill hopped onto the remaining swing, and soon they were all three whizzing through the air, whooping and laughing.

Soon Fiona tired of the activity and hopped off to join Jellybean in his pursuit of a brown bird.

Bill swung high up and suddenly let go, hurtling into the air and landing on his feet in the sand. He threw up his hands. "A perfect ten!"

"For sure!" she called.

"Now you."

"Me?"

"Yeah!" he yelled. "Jump, Misty."

"I don't think…"

"Don't think. Just jump!"

Just jump. Let go of the chains and hurl yourself into the future, next to Bill.

As the beginnings of doubt and fear crept in, she shot forward on the swing, let go of the chains, and let the exhilarating rush of freedom carry her forward.

Her landing was not a perfect ten. She tumbled forward onto the sand, rolling over on her back in a shower of grit.

Bill was at her side in a moment, eyes wide.

He gently touched her shoulder. "Are you okay?"

She blinked up at him, adrenaline still coursing through her veins, the freedom from fear still singing through her body. Fiona joined them, fingers in her mouth, and then Jellybean, sticking his wet nose in her ear.

Misty giggled and then laughed out loud until Bill joined in and even Fiona smiled around her fingers.

"Yes!" she declared. "I'm just fine."

"Whew," he said, helping her to her feet and brushing the sand out of her hair. "You scared me there for a second." His hands grazed along her hair and her cheeks, and her heart thumped madly as he bent closer. He was not going to kiss her. Not Misty Agnelli, who had run from the town and saddled him with a rascally dog only a day before.

But he was still bending, still coming closer, until he pressed his lips to hers and hers pressed back, her head tipping upward toward the crystal blue of the sky, and the sun shining warmer than she'd ever known it could.

Until the sound of running feet made them jerk apart.

Dina was jogging along, earbuds in place. She came over and greeted them with a special warm hello for Fiona.

"Bill, I don't want you to think I forgot about you. Can I come to the shop later so we can talk?"

His tongue felt slow and stupid. What would Misty make of his booking appointments with a preschool teacher? Would she know? Would she guess?

"Oh sure. Yeah. Anytime."

"That's a cute dog," Dina said to Misty. "I heard it was Lawrence Tucker's. Is he coming back soon?"

"We can only hope," she said, the joyful abandonment on her face now gone. She was back to reserved, quiet Misty.

Dina smiled and jogged away. Misty's phone rang.

Bill was not in full possession of his senses yet, his nerves still buzzing and humming from kissing Misty. Kissing her? He could not think why he had attempted such a thing. For all his easygoing charm, he was not one to strike up relationships with women. Not the kissing, "I want to hold you in my arms and feel your heart beating against mine" type of relationships.

But there he was, with his arms still aching for the feel of her, and there she was, clutching the phone as if it were a life preserver. The way she looked at him was somehow different now. Shaded with suspicion? His gut went cold. Too close. He'd come too close to letting her see.

"H-Hello?" Misty said, avoiding looking at Bill. She listened intently while he fussed over Fiona, fixing one of her hair ties until she squirmed out of his reach. Misty repocketed the phone. "Stan said he dropped Lawrence in Twin Pines. It's about…"

"Forty-five minutes north of here."

"Why is that name familiar?"

"Dunno, but it's already four o'clock, and I have to prep for tomorrow. Okay to wait?"

She agreed.

"We could get going right after church in the morning. You, uh, want to go to the service with us? It starts at eight, and there are only about twenty-five in the congregation."

Misty chewed her lip. "Oh, um…no. No, thank you. That's a nice invitation, but I'm not…you know…" She trailed off. "No, thank you."

She was not going to leap off any more swings for Bill Woodson or walk into a church full of people she didn't know.

"Sure. Let's meet at the shop at ten." He went for the confident grin. "I'll make more peanut butter sandwiches to take along."

"Okay. Sounds good."

He eventually guided Jellybean back onto the sidewalk. "About that, um, kiss. I was too forward. I apologize."

She flushed. "It's okay. These things happen."

It won't happen again. The thought took away the warmth he'd felt only a moment before.

It's a smart thing to stay away from Misty. For once in your life, why don't you try to be smart?

Twelve

Misty awoke groggy the next morning to find a small terrier tight up against her and snoring in a volume totally out of proportion to his size. However, it wasn't Jellybean's nocturnal sounds that had kept her tossing and turning throughout the night, but rather her own noisy thoughts. Misty had never been good at interpreting social situations, but she'd seen clearly the intimate connection between Dina Everly and Bill. They knew each other in a way that she and Bill did not. It was clear they had spent time together outside of the preschool pickup and drop-off.

Why not? she asked herself bitterly as she got out of bed and pulled on her clothes. Dina was young, lovely, and easy to be around. What handsome man wouldn't want that?

Jack had. Pain lanced through her chest, not so much for the loss of Jack as the humiliation of knowing the truth. As much as she wanted to blame Jack for the end of their relationship, she couldn't. He really was a great guy, and he deserved a relationship with someone like Jill.

"I love you," he'd said. "I'll always love you, but I think we're not completely compatible." Compatible with a normal, well-rounded life.

Jack enjoyed people and parties and finding the newest hot spot in town. He was a sales rep, and he honestly loved the events, the small talk, the schmoozing and flitting from conversation to conversation like a bee in search of blossoms.

He loved, in essence, the very things Misty found frightening. But she'd learned to like those things, or at least attempt to like them, for him. Wasn't that enough? To try to mold yourself into that round peg so you'd fit into someone else's life?

Unless you didn't. And you couldn't. And it was just easier to hide yourself under that bushel or bed, or behind the anonymous computer screen. In the dead silence of the empty trailer, Misty felt her own light sputtering into darkness.

You're not compatible with Bill's life either, Misty. At least she'd figured it out early this time, before she was humiliated.

Bill deserved Dina. What better pairing than with a woman who knew all about kids—a wife and mother all rolled into one?

She looked down to find Jellybean sitting at her feet, staring up at her in that vacuous way.

"What?"

The stare.

"What do you want?"

Jellybean yipped and licked her bare feet.

"All right," she said. "One song." Taking up her violin, she poured her heart into a sad melody, the dog listening raptly. When she was done, he leaped onto her lap and swabbed her chin with his tongue to catch the tears she hadn't known were falling.

"Jelly," she said, burying her face in his wiry hair. "Did you ever feel like you were a mutt in a kennel of show dogs?" The little tongue continued to soothe the tears from her face.

"I wasn't made to shine a light. I want to go home."

Again the vacant stare, or was it perhaps a compassionate look?

She steeled her resolve. There would be no falling in love here—not with this doe-eyed charmer, and not with Bill Woodson either. "We're going to find Lawrence today and reunite you, and then I'm hitting the road for San Francisco."

Jellybean cocked his head, ears perked, circled precisely three times in her lap, and sank down into a dejected bundle.

"That's not going to work, Jelly," she said, putting him on the floor and clipping him to a leash. She thought about what Ernest had said about Lawrence.

Could be he needs more than a violin teacher.

"He needs you, Jellybean, so it's take two, silver screen rescue, and...action!"

Jellybean elevated his nose in a haughty fashion and peed on the floor mat.

∽

The drive to Twin Pines was quiet. Bill squirmed in his button-up denim shirt and jeans, wishing he'd taken the time to change into a soft T-shirt. Though the barnyard boogies blared from the CD player, no one seemed in much of a mood to sing along.

Misty sat quietly, brow furrowed, until he could stand the silence no longer.

"What are you mulling over?"

"The name of the town—Twin Pines. It's so familiar."

"Is it a place from Lawrence's past? He was raised in a foster home. Could it be he was returning to see his foster parents?" Bill figured this might be a clever deduction on his part.

"No. Vivian said they have both passed away."

He jerked. "You got that out of Vivian?"

"Barely, and only after I promised to lock Jelly in the trailer while we talked."

"I'm impressed." Misty really was an incredible woman. Smart and lovely, and way out of his league.

Twin Pines boasted five thousand residents, or so the placard read as they cruised in. It was the standard California small town, with older parts that didn't match and newer sections of squished-together houses with a Mediterranean look to their stucco exteriors.

There was only one major hotel in town, so they started there, discovering quickly that cabdrivers and hotel managers shared the same policy regarding client privacy rights.

"I didn't see him in the lobby coffee area," Misty said glumly. "But that doesn't mean he isn't here."

They checked out the local grocery store and deli as they strolled along the main drag, but there was no sign of the actor anywhere. Misty headed for a small consignment shop, the window crowded with glassware, dusty books, and a wooden rocking horse. Bill couldn't figure out what might have caught her eye until she pointed to a battered violin case, open to reveal a gleaming instrument inside.

"I always have to look. You never know where you might find a missing Stradivarius. Stradivarius only made eleven hundred or so instruments, and most are accounted for. But Ernest told me about a soldier in the Korean War who found a Strad in the walls of a burned-out farmhouse. I…" She stopped, shocked.

"What is it?"

"I just remembered why I know the name Twin Pines. It's the billing address for Ernest Finn."

"The one who recommended you for the movie job?"

She nodded slowly, brow crinkled. "And when I talked to him last, he wasn't able to do his lesson due to an unexplained conflict. He called Lawrence 'old Tuck' in the course of our conversation. Does that strike you as odd?"

"Yep, like a mystery movie. Wouldn't it be an amazing plot twist if Lawrence is holing up with your student?"

She took out her phone and tapped a few buttons. "Maybe it is time for me to meet Ernest face-to-face. He lives at 110 Elmwood Drive. Do you have a GPS?"

He flushed. "Yeah, but I never figured out how to work it."

"No problem. I'll use Google Maps."

Fiona was beginning to kick the back of the driver's seat by the time they found the tiny structure at the far edge of town. Jellybean was just as eager as Fiona to tumble from the car and scamper up the graveled drive.

Misty stopped and wiped her palms on her thighs.

"Nervous?"

"He's been my friend for six years, but that's been over Skype. I come off much better via the screen than in real life. I'm going to blabber. I can feel it."

Bill wrapped an arm around her shoulders to show support. "We know you're a Skype screen star. Now it's time to get up close and personal. He's going to love you, blabber or no blabber."

She did not look convinced, but he was dead certain. How could anyone not love her mixture of earnest sincerity and bumbling efforts to do the right thing? How could Bill himself possibly not love her?

He pushed away the pesky thought and rapped on the door. An older man with a puff of white hair that matched his suspenders appeared. His mouth fell open, and his eyes rounded behind the glasses.

"Miss Agnelli?"

"Misty," she said automatically. "And you have got to be Ernest. I mean, of course you are. Who else could you be?"

"Yes," he said, pumping her hand while she introduced her fellow travelers. "I can't believe you're here. I feel like I'm in a movie or something."

Bill laughed. "We've been having similar thoughts."

"Why have you come?" Ernest said. "I've already rescheduled my lesson."

Misty smiled. "I'm not here on music business. Ernest, I don't mean to barge in, but I have an important question to ask you."

He held up a hand. "Before you ask, please come in and let me make you some tea. I don't get much company from lovely ladies and their entourages, so this is a tea-worthy moment if there ever was one." He peered through his glasses at Fiona. "And I think I've even got some cookies somewhere. You look like the kind of young lady who likes vanilla wafers, am I right?"

Fiona clung to Bill's leg and smiled.

"Okay to bring in the dog?" Bill asked. "Or should I secure him outside?"

Ernest laughed. "Oh, he's welcome here. Always has been. Please come in."

Bill shot Misty a look. *What's going on?*

She answered with a silent, *I have no idea.*

They trailed Ernest down a sunny hallway with well-worn wooden floors into a sitting room with a faded purple sofa and two overstuffed chairs. Rows of books crammed the room's shelves, and Bill noticed a black-and-white wedding photo of a dashing Ernest and his shyly smiling bride. Two old Chihuahuas scuttled out from under the sofa and began a merry game of chase with Jellybean.

Fiona chuckled once, a small, happy sound sweeter than a Christmas bell. Bill wanted to pump his fist in the air. Two sounds in one week. Even if he was going to say goodbye to Misty and his business in short order, at least that was a positive sign. Fiona was feeling more comfortable, safer. But what if he had to close the shop and move her again? Where would they go? And how long would it take before he heard the hum and giggle of a secure child once more?

Fiona set about rolling a tennis ball and watching the three dogs set off in hot pursuit, furry planets whizzing around in their own frantic orbits.

"Well, that should keep them busy for a while," Ernest said, returning from the kitchen with a tray, glasses of iced tea, and a bowl of vanilla wafers.

Misty gestured. "This room is exactly like I've seen on Skype every week for the past six years. I feel like I've stepped through the looking glass."

"Me too," Ernest said. "And may I note that you are even prettier in person?"

"Thank you," Misty said, spots of pink appearing on her cheeks, like Bill's perfect candy roses against satiny white chocolate. "It's... special to meet someone face-to-face, isn't it?"

Ernest saluted her with his glass of tea. "A toast to face-to-face friends."

They clinked glasses and sipped.

He went to a shelf in a crammed china cupboard and set out a box of Chocolate Heaven truffles. Bill and Misty exchanged a look.

"Ernest, I have to ask that question now, if you don't mind."

He sighed. "Ask away. I think I might have an idea why you're here."

Misty set down her glass. "Did you cancel our lesson because you had an unexpected houseguest?"

Ernest sighed. "Yes."

Bill sat up straighter. They'd actually figured it out? Found the elusive actor? Unbelievable.

"I knew it," Misty chortled. "Lawrence is here, isn't he?"

The expression on Ernest's weathered face put a tinge of doubt over Bill's optimism.

"No," Ernest said. "I'm sorry to say he is not."

Thirteen

Misty's hope turned to disappointment before Ernest finished his sentence. So much for the detective work.

"Oh, I was sure he was hiding out here."

"He was, but he left this morning before I got up." Ernest sighed. "Tuck was always one for the mysterious exit and entrance."

"So he was here? And you're friends?" Bill asked.

"Friends," Ernest agreed. "I've known Tuck since he was a sixteen-year-old spotty-faced kid. We lived up north in a small town close to Fresno called Benson. The wife and I owned a convenience store there. Tuck came to live in Benson with a foster family—one of several he'd been in, I gathered."

"How sad," Misty said.

"His mom gave birth at age fifteen and tried to raise him as best she could with the help of her grandmother, but after Granny died, she just couldn't take it." Ernest shook his head. "She left him at his kindergarten class one day and never came back. Tuck went into foster care at age five."

An ache started up inside Misty when she imagined Lawrence's abandonment. At five years old, she was hiding under her father's bed, praying he wouldn't die. But there had been others there coaxing her out, reassuring her and reminding her that she was loved dearly by her family and by God. Through all the lonely periods in her life, she'd had her family, and she'd had God. Lawrence had no one to reassure him, no arms waiting to hug him or knees bent in prayer for him. "I didn't know that, Ernest."

"He lived up and down the coast with various families, stayed in Albatross for a while too, but he liked me and the missus for some reason. Used to come in when he lived close and read all the movie magazines and gossip rags from cover to cover. We never minded. Even went camping together once. Me and the missus were bigtime campers." Ernest chuckled. "Man, that Tuck could spin some whoppers. He'd tell me one day that his real daddy was a spy for the navy, and the next that his pop was a missionary in Guatemala."

Misty nodded. "I figured some of his stories had to be made up."

Ernest's smile dimmed. "Sad part was, seemed like Tuck didn't know the difference after a while, like he preferred the lies because they were better than his real life."

"I can read people, study them, extract their motivations for my own purposes. It's clinical in a way," he'd said. He wandered through life reading people as if they were interesting scripts. *"You are a woman in hiding,"* he'd told her. The comment awakened an uneasy tide.

Did she do the same? Watch people, study them from her safe hidey-hole?

"He was down in the dumps when he showed up at my place two days ago," Ernest was saying. "Said there was some trouble on the film set, and he was getting too old. His agent was having a hard time finding him jobs."

The three dogs whizzed through the room, followed by a beaming Fiona.

Ernest eyed them sadly. "Old Tuck said even Jellybean didn't like him anymore."

Bill drank some tea. "So your connection to Lawrence—is that how Misty got involved in the movie?"

Misty gave him a halfhearted frown. "You didn't tell me you knew the star of the film."

He laughed. "Yeah. Tuck likes to stick with the lies, so I don't blab to folks about our connection. When he told me the movie was gonna be shot in Albatross and they were looking for a violin teacher, why, naturally, I supplied Lawrence your name."

"Naturally," Misty said. "But I'm afraid that didn't work out too well."

Ernest patted her arm. "Sure it did. You got to know Tuck, and you care enough about him to come all this way looking for him. No one else would do that."

She felt a stab of guilt. "I'm afraid it's not that altruistic. The film means a lot to the town. If he doesn't come back, the movie people will pack up and leave along with all the potential visitors."

"Hmm…I see. I wish I could tell you where he's gone, but I just don't know."

"Did he take a taxi? Or the bus?" Bill asked.

"Dunno. He vamoosed before I got up this morning, leaving this candy behind."

Misty groaned. "Now how are we going to find him?"

"I don't know what to tell you about the detective stuff, but I suspect he may call me, and I'll do my best to send him in your direction. I promise."

They stood, and Bill collected Fiona.

Misty grasped Ernest's arthritic hands in hers. They were warm and soft, these hands that labored to pluck at the strings. She knew the visit had altered things between them, deepened their friendship and knitted a tighter connection between them. The power of it amazed her. How could such a simple thing as a quick talk and a grasping of hands change so much?

"Thank you, Ernest."

"Anytime, Miss Agnelli. Say, maybe if you're in town a while, we could do a real lesson in the same room. Whaddaya say?" His eyes sparkled.

The idea tickled inside her, urging her to step up, step out. But at what cost? People brought disappointment and heartache, broken hearts and battered emotions. People left you in kindergarten classes and under beds and with newly purchased dresses that would never be worn, invited to weddings for people for whom couplehood was natural and right. She felt Bill's gaze searching her face.

"I'm going home in the next week, as soon as I can get Lawrence back to the set," she said firmly, "but we can continue our lessons over Skype."

"Sure, okay," Ernest said, letting go of her fingers, some of the animation draining from his face.

*Let your light shine…*the phrase beat inside her heart like the insistent tapping of a snare drum. But surely Jesus meant that for brilliant preachers thundering in the pulpit or stalwart missionaries tending to the masses. Could it be that Misty's light was a little flicker meant to show love to an elderly man? Was that what God wanted her to do with her musical passion? Could it be that small and that immense?

"But I will probably come back every couple months," she blurted out. "I mean, to visit Bill and bring Nana Bett. She loves Albatross. Maybe we could get together then and do a lesson."

Ernest's face dawned in a smile that rivaled the most beautiful sunrise. His warmth seeped right into her as he gave her hands another squeeze. "That would be wonderful," he said, blinking. "Just wonderful."

His two dogs yapped and scrambled over his feet.

"Gummy, you're a menace," Ernest said when he managed to catch the nearest one. "And you're no better, Juju."

"Unusual names," Bill said.

Ernest smiled. "The missus always named our pets after candies. She had a ferocious sweet tooth. Doc said she wasn't to be eating treats, but I'd find her candy wrappers stuffed down in the recliner cushions. I didn't say anything. Sweets made her happy, and that made me happy." He scratched the captured dog behind the ears. "This is Gumdrop, and that one licking your shoe is Jujube."

Bill and Misty locked eyes.

"Ernest," Misty said, "Jellybean used to be your dog, didn't he?"

"Never really anyone's dog," Ernest said. "He has too much independence for that. Showed up in our tent one time when we were camping, and we took him in even though Jeannie was getting ready to start treatments at the time. She never could turn away an animal in need, and I never could say no to anything she had her heart set on. Jelly made her laugh like crazy." A mixture of joy and pain was written on Ernest's face. "Tuck visited at Jeannie's funeral, and he offered to take Jellybean. It was okay by me, as three dogs was a lot for an old man."

Misty sighed. "I should have known the story about saving the dog from a frozen lake was not the truth."

Ernest kissed Gummy on the top of his head and smoothed a wrinkled hand over his back. "It's truth enough to make Tuck feel special, and that's all he's really ever wanted. To be special to someone."

To be special to someone. It was a tune with which Misty was all too familiar.

She hugged Ernest and kissed his stubbly cheek.

"We'll make arrangements to see each other soon. It really was good to meet you, Ernest."

He grinned. "Likewise."

Bill was not able to glean anything from the bus station or the cabdrivers, so there was nothing to be done but head back to

Albatross. After they settled at home and spent a quiet afternoon and dinner hour, and Fiona had drifted off to sleep, he wandered the tiny shop, tidying up and ignoring the pile of bills accumulating near the phone. They would not be denied much longer. Doing an extra set of push-ups enabled him to put the bills out of his mind and fall into a restless slumber.

And then, quite suddenly, it was Monday.

He let Fiona sleep and crept downstairs to find the message light beeping on his answering machine. The call must have come sometime in the night.

"It's Yolanda, Mr. Wilson's assistant." The woman leaving a message sounded harried and breathless. "Sorry to call on late notice, but can you deliver six dozen chocolates to the set Monday at noon? Mr. Wilson has to put on a dog and pony...I mean, entertain a private investor who's coming to tour the set. We'll pay whatever you want as long as it's not over a hundred bucks, but be here at noon, okay?" There was a pause. "Please?"

Bill checked the time. Seven thirty. If he got cracking immediately, with Gunther's help, he would just make it. Tying on an apron, he whistled a barnyard boogie tune. Business. Money in the till. Providing for Fiona. Succeeding.

He set to work on tempering the chocolate, and by seven forty-five, the caramel was in progress. Next would be a nice light strawberry filling that would pair beautifully with a dark chocolate shell.

Time ticked on, and he heard the bell on the door jingle. He exhaled in relief. Fiona would be awakening soon, and he desperately needed the help of his surly employee.

Gunther pushed on in. "Stoppin' in to tell you I cain't come in, least until later."

"What's wrong?"

"Ah, somethin' with Lunk. He's in the truck waiting. Got out again last night and didn't drag his sorry self home until after midnight. Ain't eating this morning. Never passed up a meal in all the time I known him. Gotta take him to the doctor."

As much as Bill wanted to protest, he knew that Lunk was family to Gunther, a man with no wife or children. Gunther consistently declined Bill's invitations to join him and Fiona for church, dinner, and even an early morning cup of coffee, so Lunk was his life. "Sure. Come on in when you can. I'll say a prayer for Lunk."

Gunther raised a grizzled eyebrow. "Pray?" He shifted uneasily. "People pray for dogs?"

"I don't know about other people," Bill said with a smile. "But I do."

Gunther looked at his shoes. "Oh…well, okay then." He took off his hat and rubbed a circle on the top of his speckled scalp. "That's nice of you."

Bill nodded. "I know how important Lunk is to you."

"Yeah, well, he's a lazy lout and he don't know any tricks at all, but I got a soft spot for him, which shows I ain't got no sense at all." More head scratching. "Hey, by the way, your mum called with that toffee recipe. I wrote it all down for you." He paused. "But, uh, you know, my, er, handwriting is terrible, so I'll probably just have to tell you what it says."

Bill could not quite look at his friend. Humiliation, gratitude, affection all swirled together in his gut, but most prominent was the ever-present mountain of shame. When he finally raised his gaze again, Gunther was gone. Bill silenced the anxiety building inside and said a prayer for Lunk and Gunther. He'd gotten to "Amen" when another peal of bells ushered in Misty, holding tight to Jellybean.

"I wondered if I can leave Jelly here for a few hours. I'm going to drive back to Twin Pines and ask the neighbors on Ernest's street if they saw Lawrence leave." Her mouth crimped. "Frankly, I'm not sure if that info will help me find him or not, but I don't know what else to do."

Bill smiled.

"What? Why are you smiling?"

"Because on behalf of the town of Albatross and myself, I'm grateful."

"Why? Why would you be grateful? I caused the whole 'Lawrence flees town' scenario when I called in Phyllis the dog trainer."

"But now you're doing your best to fix it, and even though you don't like people or small towns, you're hauling yourself right out in the middle of both."

She grimaced. "Don't remind me. If there was a way to fix this through Skype, I'd be all over it. My palms are already sweaty." As if to confirm, Jellybean licked her fingers. She looked around. "Expecting some customers today?"

Bill explained about the order, gratified to see a smile light her face.

"Oh, that's great. Is Gunther coming in to help?"

He continued to stir the chocolate. "Lunk's sick. Gunther's going to be gone for a while."

Misty opened the side door and let Jellybean outside. "Don't eat anything or dig an escape tunnel, do you hear me?" she called as Jellybean scampered away. Then she returned, washed her hands, grabbed Gunther's apron, tying it around her slender middle, and tucked her hair into a white paper hat.

Bill stared, an electric tingle starting up his arm as she brushed by him into the kitchen area.

"What are you doing?" he asked.

"You need help to get those truffles done and delivered by noon," she said, avoiding looking at him.

He could not explain his surge of happiness. "So you want to help? Really? What about Twin Pines?"

"A couple hours won't make a difference." She rested her hands on her hips. "What should I do?"

He pulled his mind back to the task at hand. "If you could make the strawberry cream, that would be great."

She chewed a lip. "I can do it if you've got the recipe."

He tapped a finger to his temple. "I have it all up here. I'll tell you what to do."

She grabbed a spatula and saluted. "Carry on, Chef Bill."

He laughed and began to guide her through the process of warming the frozen berries and pureeing them in the blender. Misty worked with all the precision of a surgeon in an operating room. Her fingers danced nimbly over the simmering pot of puree, straining out the seeds through the sieve, adding the butter, salt, and flour until she had made a mouthwatering pink filling.

"Now the finishing touch," he said. "Chop up some freeze-dried strawberries and fold them in before you chill it down in the fridge."

Her eyes, as rich and glossy as the ganache, opened wide in surprise. "Never would have thought of that."

"Candy is my life," he joked.

"Genius," she said, chopping the berries.

"I wish," he said, but the comment thrilled him nonetheless.

Fiona padded into the kitchen, hair wild, a book tucked under her arm. There was a smear of jam on her chin from her morning toast. She clutched a sparkly wand with a foam star on the end.

"Hey, Fee. Oh, that's right. Today is your special show, isn't it?"

Fiona nodded.

"She's going to be a snowflake in the winter recital," Bill explained. "Miss Dina says she's an amazing twirler."

"Let's see," Misty encouraged. "Can you do a twirl?"

Fiona lifted her arms, dropping the book, and executed a jerky turn, smiling at the applause from Misty and Bill.

"Bravo," Bill said, eyeing the clock. " She has to get to school at nine. Normally, Gunther would mind the shop while I ran her over there." He frowned at the digital clock. "Oh, man. Almost eight thirty already."

Misty wiped her hands on her apron. "I can get you to school, Fiona, but let's brush your hair first, okay?"

Fiona shot her a doubtful look.

"She hates having her hair brushed," Bill said under his breath.

Misty raised an eyebrow at Fiona. "If you're going to be a snowflake, you have to look your best."

Fiona considered for a moment, and then she put her wand on her chair, nodded, and trekked back toward the stairs. Misty hung up her apron and followed.

"Hey…uh, I sure do appreciate this," Bill said. "I mean, you don't have to do the child care thing."

Misty cocked her head, her bangs falling over her forehead. "I'm happy to do it. I've always liked hanging out with kids. They never seem to mind if I'm clumsy or awkward."

"You aren't either of those things to me." Immediately, his stomach dropped. What had he just said? And why? It was the truth—he couldn't deny it. He didn't see awkwardness in Misty, only earnestness. Where she stumbled, he felt only the desire to help her up, to be the one whose hand she grasped, whose shoulder she leaned on.

Crazy thoughts. He could not think of anything to say to dilute the emotion in his last remark. She watched him, frozen, before she ducked her chin, mumbled something he could not make out, and trotted up the steps after Fiona.

She's leaving at the end of the week, remember? He began reaching for the ingredients to start on the next recipe.

Bill Woodson, just make your candy and keep your mouth shut.

Fourteen

Misty was satisfied with the neat pigtails she'd achieved on Fiona. She'd had to carefully comb through many tangles and balled-up bits in the back, but they'd managed to get the job done. Now two blond crescents of hair were secured on either side of her plump cheeks, a white bow pinned on each one.

Misty held her up to the mirror, and Fiona tossed her head from side to side to set the pigtails in motion. She smiled.

Job well done, Misty.

"Okay, let's get your wand from the kitchen, and I'll take you to school."

Fiona pounded down the stairs into the kitchen, where Bill was engrossed in some confectionary magic whereby he was covering white filling with robes of silken chocolate.

Fiona peered over the edge of the table, frowning.

"Where's Fiona's wand?" Misty said, looking under the table. "Did you move it?"

Bill jerked his attention away from the candy making. "What? I haven't left this spot."

"It's gone." Misty turned a slow circle, a feeling of dread gathering in her stomach. "Uh-oh. I must not have closed the door to the yard all the way." She and Bill came to the same conclusion at the very same moment.

"Jellybean!" they hollered in unison, dashing out into the backyard.

Outside, the terrier froze as if in a spotlight when they rounded on him, the wand clamped in his teeth.

Fiona let out a soft whimper.

"Drop it!" Misty called.

Jellybean's tail arced into a *C* and began to wag in a playful pendulum.

"This isn't a game," Misty said severely. "Drop that right now."

It could not be an impish grin that graced the thin, whiskered mouth. Misty had read somewhere that dogs did not show human emotion, yet Jellybean appeared to do just that before he sprinted into action, Bill in pursuit.

They made a speeding circle around the yard. Misty tried to cut Jellybean off at the far end of the yard, but there was no stopping the zany dog who easily outstripped both of them, dodging between legs and zigzagging around outstretched arms with his prize in his mouth.

No amount of yelling made the slightest difference. Neither did Misty's idea to offer one of the dog treats she'd purchased after she'd seen how they worked for Phyllis the trainer.

Jellybean ignored the offered treat as he gleefully zoomed around the yard. When they all stopped to pant and catch their breath, Misty noticed that Fiona was crying.

She knelt in front of the child. "It's okay. I'm going to get that wand from Jellybean. Don't you worry. He's going to get tired soon."

But Jellybean did not look at all tired, the clockwork tail marking time until his next burst of activity would commence.

Bill was flushed red. "That dog is the worst-behaved animal I've ever met, and that includes a mule I once worked with. He earned the name of Crank honestly." He checked his watch, shoving a hand through his hair. "I can't chase this dog around all morning. Maybe we should take Fiona to preschool without the wand."

Tears leaked out of the little girl's eyes.

"I know how to do it," Misty said, in a moment of inspiration. "How did we get him out of the tank?"

Bill's face lit up. "Do you have your violin handy?"

"It's in the car." She sprinted to her trunk and brought back her instrument. "Okay, Bill. Get ready for the grab."

"I'm on it."

Misty played a soft peal of Bach's Chaconne. Jellybean stiffened, ears perked. As she continued to stroke the bow over the strings, the dog crept closer and closer. When she was twenty measures in, Jellybean plopped himself at her feet, not reacting in the slightest when Bill took the wand from his mouth.

"Yes!" he crowed, but Misty was captivated by something else. Fiona was staring, arms outstretched toward Misty's violin.

"Do you like the music, Fiona?" Misty asked.

She nodded.

"Would you like to play?"

Fiona looked Misty full in the face. "Uh-huh," she said.

Though joy danced inside her as she knew it must be doing in Bill, she was careful not to react as she knelt down and held the instrument for Fiona.

"Your chin goes here," she said, "but I'll bring you a smaller violin later if you want. For now, let's rest it on your shoulder." When the violin was balanced, she curled Fiona's fingers over the bow, and together they stroked the bow over the strings. With the tiny fingers tucked inside her own, they played a tentative scale.

When the first note came, Jellybean barked his approval. At the end of the scale, he rolled on his back and wriggled. Misty felt like doing the same.

Fiona was satisfied with her first performance and relinquished the instrument to Misty.

Bill stood frozen, an incongruous picture of a burly man holding a sparkly wand, a look of rapture on his face as if he had witnessed something far more momentous than a child's first attempt on an instrument.

"You know, Bill, I think I was wrong," Misty said after a beat. "Maybe Fiona is ready to learn the violin."

"Yeah," he whispered. "Maybe so. Can you…" He swallowed. "Will you teach her?"

Was he asking her to stay? Implying that he wanted Misty to stick around? The thought warmed her until the voice of doubt rose up.

It's not you he wants. It's help for his daughter. It could not be you.

No, she thought sadly. *Surely not.* "We can work out something for Fiona after I leave," she said. "She will need direct teaching. Skype won't do for a young student like her. I can get you a referral for someone local."

Someone local. Someone charming and witty. Someone who was not paralyzed by rejection. Someone who was not Misty Agnelli.

"Come on, Fiona," she said, forcing a bright smile. "Let's go to school."

As Misty walked Fiona along the sidewalk, breathing in the sea-scented air, her own sense of panic ebbed slowly away. Why had she freaked out exactly? Bill Woodson liked her—maybe more than liked her. He'd encouraged…no, directly invited her to be involved in his life and Fiona's. Her spirit sang at the prospect.

And then she recalled how she'd practically bolted from his shop. But what if she allowed herself a moment to consider that she was worth pursuing? How amazing would it be if Bill really didn't see her awkwardness and social ineptitude? His words rang in her ears.

"You aren't either of those things to me."

What if she dared to believe that Bill saw a light in her that she didn't see in herself? What if that was the truth?

What if she was a light to Bill and Fiona?

They reached the preschool before she'd come to a conclusion of any kind. The place was abuzz with activity, full of kids with wands similar to Fiona's, alternately waving them around and using them as swords or lightsabers. She was happy to see Fiona scurry immediately into the gang, waving her wand with gusto. A parent was tacking a paper garland around a small raised platform that had been erected for the recital. Another was setting up several rows of folding chairs.

Dina caught sight of Misty as she was about to leave, and waved.

"Hi." She frowned. "Where's Bill?"

Not Mr. Woodson or Fiona's dad. Bill. The familiarity of it poked at Misty. Just friends?

"He has a delivery. He'll be here in time for the show."

"Oh. Okay," she said. "I know he wouldn't miss it. We'd love for you to come too."

But Misty was already hurrying from the school, eager to get back.

Bill tried not to stare too much at Misty as she rolled the chilled strawberry filling into perfect balls, but it was so cute the way her nose wrinkled in concentration and she clamped her lower lip between her teeth. Thanks to her help, they were ready at ten minutes after eleven to load the cardboard boxes into the coolers, sliding them into the back of Bill's van.

He held up a palm.

Misty was perplexed. "Stop?"

"No. High five." He laughed.

"Oh, right." She palm slapped him with a giggle.

"Thanks to you, I'm going to make this delivery on time, and Fiona has added to her spoken repertoire."

Misty slapped him a follow-up high five. "That part deserves another five."

"We'll make it ten then." He could not wipe the grin off his face. "The psychologist said it would probably be like that, a few words here or there as she felt better about things. That's good, because if she broke into a speech or something, I'd probably have a heart attack." Gunther met them in the parking lot.

"Lunk's okay," he said. "Just suffering from exhaustion. Dunno where he made off to last night, but it tuckered him out. He'll be right as rain, 'cept the doc said he needs to lose some weight, so he's got some diet food. Smells terrible. Glad I don't have to eat it."

"Poor Lunk," Misty said.

"Hope he learns a lesson this time."

Bill told Gunther about the movie set delivery. Misty agreed to accompany him before she set off for Twin Pines.

"I'll mind the store while you're gone," Gunther said.

"Keep an eye on Jellybean, okay?" Bill said. "He's already made off with a magic wand today, and I think he's back to working on his tunnel."

"Not like we're gonna get any customers anyway," Gunther said, waving a weary hand and trudging into the shop.

They drove to the movie set and found the harried Yolanda, who had left the message. She was still frazzled but doing her best to hide it. She pumped both their hands and led them to a linen-covered table set up under a canopy where there was a pitcher full of ice water with lemon slices and a half dozen glasses. "I'm so relieved," she said. "Nothing has gone right on this movie since

day one. Now we've got Todd Bannington wanting to see the set."
She dropped her volume to a dramatic whisper. "He's a private
investor on the film. If he pulls out, we're in an even worse mess
than before."

A worse mess than having your star missing? Bill puzzled over
that one.

Yolanda leaned closer. "Have you found Mr. Tucker yet?"

"No, but we're getting closer," Bill said when Misty did not
answer. "Shouldn't be long now, right, Misty?"

"Uh, right. Not long. We hope."

Yolanda let loose with a gusty sigh. "Great. Maybe I will still
have a job next week, then. I've got a kid who needs braces like you
wouldn't believe. He looks like a crocodile with freckles."

With a valiant effort, Bill did not laugh. Misty busied herself
arranging napkins on the table, but he saw her lips pressed together,
possibly to contain a giggle.

"There they are now," Yolanda said, eyeing a BMW pulling to a
stop near the trailers. "It's showtime. Be right back."

He set out the candies on long silver trays and was filled with
satisfaction to see the mouthwatering chocolate gems. Chocolate
making would never leave him rich or paint him as a success in
his father's estimation, but his fruits made people happy, if only
for a moment.

What was a moment of sweetness worth? He thought of the
impact a single word from Fiona had on him, the thrill he got from
hearing Misty play her violin, the comfort he felt from a single
prayer. He considered how supremely delighted Jellybean was at
the prospect of a quick belly scratch or a moth to chase after. What
was a moment of sweetness worth?

Everything, he thought.

Misty was already edging away toward the van when the
group of well-dressed men approached. He followed, intending
to stay with Misty until the mucky-mucks were done sampling the

chocolates and he could retrieve his trays. Though he did not shy away from people generally, this time he figured he'd take a clue from Misty and err on the side of discretion.

He got to the van first and opened the passenger door for her. She blushed and rested her hand on his arm, giving him another rush of sweetness.

"Misty?" a voice called out from behind them.

It was one of the well-dressed men, with neatly styled hair, dress pants, and a sport jacket over his shirt.

"Misty Agnelli?" the man repeated, breaking into a smile as he came closer. "I thought that was you. Come here and give me a hug."

Bill watched as Misty's face turned a brilliant shade of pink. The man caught her up in an embrace that lifted her feet off the ground. When he kissed her cheek, Bill's jaw clenched.

The man put her down. "I am so glad to see you. I didn't know you were working in the area."

"Yes," Misty said faintly. "Uh…Bill, this is Jack."

Jack. From the Jack and Jill connection. Jack, the man who had loved Misty.

That Jack.

Fifteen

The shock washed over Misty like a rogue wave.

Jack was staring at her with wide blue eyes, resplendent in his nice clothes and leather wing tips.

"What...what are you doing here?"

"Todd Bannington's an entrepreneur friend of mine. I help him with real estate deals now and then. He asked me to come along with him on this set visit since he's a major investor. There have been rumors that the shoot's falling apart, that the star walked off and isn't coming back."

"He's coming back," Misty blurted. "I mean, by Friday. I'm sure he'll be back by Friday."

Jack cocked his head in that way he'd always done, a mixture of boy next door and corporate CEO. "What's your role here, Misty?"

"I'm..." And then her words floated away like a life preserver tossed just out of reach. The weight of his gaze stripped away her power to say anything intelligible.

"She's the violin tutor and assistant to the star, Lawrence Tucker," Bill put in.

"Oh, hey," Jack said, extending his hand. "Rude of me not to introduce myself. Jack Golding."

"Bill Woodson."

"Do you work on the set too?"

"I run a chocolate shop." Bill said it with his chin up. He stood ramrod straight, a good three inches taller than Jack.

Jack's companion called to him.

"I'd better get back," Jack said. He took Misty's hand. "We're staying over at the Lady Bug."

"The Lady Bird," Bill corrected.

He laughed. "I was close." His hands caressed Misty's. "Since you're in town, why don't we have dinner tonight?"

Misty paled and then flushed hot again. "I'm sure Jill will want to have dinner with you. They have such good food at the Lady Bird, I've been told. She'll love it."

Jack blew out a breath. "We're actually taking a break from each other right now."

Misty's mouth actually dropped open before she could stop it. "Oh."

He offered a regretful smile. "These things happen. Nice to meet you, Bill. I'll come visit your shop if I have time." He dropped a quick kiss on Misty's cheek, and she caught his signature musky aftershave. "I'll call you about dinner. Still have the same cell number?"

She nodded. Both Bill and Jack moved to close the door as Misty got into the passenger seat. Bill got there first, but Misty was already reaching for it herself by that time. His push and her pull combined, and Misty knocked her forehead against the glass with a thunk.

Jack and Bill both bent to peer in concern through the window.

"Are you okay?" they asked in muffled unison.

She offered a cheery smile through the pain pounding in her forehead. It must have been a convincing act, because Jack trotted away toward Bannington and the chocolates.

Bill walked around the van, opened his door, and climbed inside. He jabbed the key in the ignition. "I'll come back for the platters later." He stopped when he got a good look at her. "Oh, man. You have a bump on your forehead."

She clapped a hand there and said, "Typical Misty move."

He took the road back to town. "We'll get an ice pack on that back at the shop."

Happy to stew in embarrassed silence, Misty marked off the distance to the rhythmical throbbing in her head.

Back at Chocolate Heaven, they said hello to Gunther and settled into the rusted patio chairs after Bill provided a plastic bag full of ice. Jellybean gave Misty's shoes a thorough sniffing before he returned to the halfway-devoured bone she'd given him the day before, which was guaranteed to last three weeks.

Thoughts chased themselves around in her mind. Jack. Here in Albatross. No longer with Jill. It was unbelievable. Jill was perfect, the best companion for a man like Jack. How could they have broken up?

She saw from under the edge of the ice pack that Bill was staring at her.

"I guess he, er, caught you by surprise. Jack, I mean." He rubbed a palm on the thigh of his jeans.

"For sure. I had no idea he was in town or that he had anything to do with the movie biz."

Bill drummed his fingers on the table. "And he's single again."

"That was the biggest shocker of all."

Bill folded and then unfolded his arms. "Are you...going to meet him for dinner? You're right, the Lady Bird does have great food." He scraped a bit of dirt off the patio table. "Vivian is famous for her biscuits. Gunther orders them regularly, and I suspect he shares them with Lunk."

Meet Jack? The suddenly single love of her life? Oh, how she'd hoped for the weeks following their breakup that Jack would realize he'd made a mistake with Jill. Misty had it all imagined in her mind right down to the musical score. He would beg her forgiveness, tell her it was the worst mistake of his life, cue the overture. Now here it was, her one-in-a-million chance to reunite with him.

"No," she said. "I'm not going to meet him for dinner."

Bill blinked. "Why not?"

She put down the ice pack and walked to the small patch of clematis that was doing its best to smother the leaning split rail fence. Out behind the yard was a grass-filled lot where Fiona liked to watch for bunnies and pick whatever interesting plants she could find to make a weed bouquet. Misty had one Fiona had given her in an empty pickle jar in the trailer. *Flowers finer than any florist's offerings*, Misty thought.

Why not? That was the question hanging in the air. She could feel Bill just behind her, patiently waiting for an answer.

She turned toward him. "I won't go to dinner with Jack because…" The sound of waves carried on the breeze. "Because I don't want to be a square peg in his round-hole life." *There was a suitably weird reply,* she thought ruefully. She was surprised to find that Bill did not look at all perplexed. Instead, his face was peaceful.

"I understand," he said. Then his hands were on her shoulders, toying with her hair. "I like square pegs. They're my favorite kind." His smile was tender.

She waited for the rush of nerves, the thick weight of anxiety to crash down on her at his proximity, but she felt nothing but lightness and warmth at his touch, as she had when they'd embraced at the park. She looked into the bottle-green eyes, the strong profile topped by a ten-dollar haircut, the arms covered in a well-worn T-shirt with a splotch of chocolate just above the pocket. He really did like Misty "Square Peg" Agnelli, not in spite of her oddities, but because of them.

Light seemed to flood her insides. In a dreamlike state, she watched him lean down and press his mouth to hers. How right it felt, how perfectly right. She tentatively rested her hand on the back of his neck, enjoying the prickliness of his hair, the strong solidity of his head.

Gunther called from the back door, causing them to jump apart. She thought there might be a smile on his perpetually scowling mouth, but she couldn't tell for sure.

"Phone call for you, Bill."

Bill trotted to grab the phone, which extended in a curled cord from the kitchen. "Hello?" Whatever was said on the other end snuffed out the joy that had shone on his face a moment before like a candle doused by a strong wind.

"What? But I've got the invitation right here." He reached inside and snatched a paper from the bulletin board. "It says two thirty."

She could not hear what was said to Bill, but he mumbled something, head bowed, and hung up.

Defeat was written in every line of his body.

"What is it, Bill?" she asked.

At first, he did not answer.

"Bill?" she tried again, touching his arm.

Mouth tight, he handed her the paper. "Read it."

She expected it to be something horrible, but it was nothing more than a sweet invitation to the winter recital at Fiona's school, complete with a cute font and an adorable snowflake graphic. "I don't understand."

"Here," he said, jabbing a finger. "What does that part say?"

"We're inviting all of our friends and family to the winter recital to be performed at Happy Days Preschool on January fifteenth at…" Her voice trailed off. "Oh no! It says ten thirty a.m." The time was now closing in on one o'clock.

"Dina tried to call, but I forgot my cell phone." Bill's face was ashen.

"It was a simple mistake," Misty said.

He started to speak but then clamped his lips together. "I have to go get her."

"I'll come." Twin Pines would have to wait.

She wasn't sure he heard her, so she scurried to keep up with him as he raced to the van and they drove the three blocks to the preschool. What had gone wrong? She couldn't figure it out.

The stage was empty, the kids playing in the yard, awaiting parent pickup. Fiona was sitting by herself looking at a book.

Dina looked up from wiping the table, her expression sympathetic. "Don't worry. I took some great pictures for you," she said to Bill. "Fiona did a super job on her twirling."

He didn't answer. Head bowed, he went to Fiona and knelt down next to her.

"I'm so sorry I didn't come for your show."

She didn't look up at him but turned the page and stared at the pictures.

"Fee, I'm really, really sorry."

Misty heard the break in Bill's voice, and it made her breath catch.

Dina approached. "Fiona, remember how we practiced in school the 'cleanup'? When someone does something wrong, they say, "I'm sorry," and we say, "That's okay." Your Uncle Bill is very sorry. Can you show him it's okay? If you can't use your words, can you nod your head?"

Fiona cast a blank look at Bill. Then she returned her attention to her book. Everything in Misty wanted to run to Bill and put her arms around him, but it would add to the mountain of feelings he was experiencing at that moment, so she held herself in place.

Eventually, he got up, and Dina handed Fiona her magic wand and her papers. Fiona would not take Bill's hand as they went back to the van, but she accepted Misty's.

They rode back to Chocolate Heaven in silence, Misty still not completely taking it all in. He'd missed a show, gotten caught up in the details of his business, or just misread the time. It would pass. She hated to see him beat himself up over a small mistake.

At the shop, Misty helped Fiona out of the car and took her inside. The child went immediately to her little chair, gathering up a stack of books on her lap.

Bill stood on the porch, staring.

"Kids don't hold on to these things, Bill. She will forget about it. Probably by tomorrow."

"I won't," he said.

"It was a mistake—anyone could have made it."

"No, not anyone."

"You were busy. You scanned the invitation quickly. You have a lot on your mind."

He rounded on her, something hard and bleak shining in his eyes. "You don't know, do you?"

"Know what?"

He rubbed a hand over his face. "Gunther knows. And Dina. Heck, probably the whole town knows."

"Knows what, Bill? What are you talking about?"

He took the crumpled invitation from his pocket. "It wasn't a mistake. I thought it said two thirty, not ten thirty."

"Anyone could have…" she started again.

"No. Not anyone. Just me." His tone was anguished, hands balled into fists. "I thought it said two thirty because I can't read."

She stared. He saw the meaning of his pronouncement slowly unrolling across her face. First disbelief and then recognition as she thought back on all the things she'd probably noticed but not quite acknowledged.

"You…you can't read?"

"No. I've been trying to learn all my life." He could not believe he was talking about his deepest shame with the woman he desperately wanted to respect him, a woman who made him feel whole.

Her mouth opened and closed. "I...I didn't know."

"That's because I'm a master at covering up. I've had years, decades of practice. Dina's been trying to help me learn, giving me worksheets and stuff." He laughed—a bitter, angry sound he didn't recognize as his own voice. "Isn't that rich? Trying to master preschool reading so I can be one step ahead of a three-year-old? 'Good job, Bill. Here's a smiley face sticker. I'm so proud of you. Why don't you sit down and play with the Play-Doh too?'"

"Don't, Bill. You're trying. That's the important thing, right?"

Oh, the hopeful tone, how she desperately wanted to see the light shining in the gloom. But there wasn't any. There never had been. "No," he said. "It's not important at all. I've been failing since I was Fiona's age. In grade school, in middle school. Finally, in high school I figured out how to fake it, ask my buddies to write my papers for me and tell me what the books were about, until I dropped out. A couple of them even helped me practice the driving test questions so I could get my license."

"But surely—"

"But surely what?" he snapped. "Surely a fully grown man couldn't have gotten through his life without knowing how to read? Surely an adult should be able to go into a restaurant without ordering a hamburger every time rather than trying to read the menu? Surely a fully grown man can write a sign for his own business and not have to have his employee do it?" His voice was nearly a shout, but he couldn't control himself. All the anger and shame and humiliation came pouring out in a volley of self-loathing.

She was staring at him, lip caught between her teeth.

"And surely the dumb brother didn't go and wind up being the guardian of a bright little kid when the smart brother went and got himself killed?" His breath came in hot bursts, each one an effort.

"Oh, Bill," she said, taking a step toward him.

He moved away. Misty did not deserve to be shouted at, but he would rather push her away than have her do an about-face because he was illiterate. He couldn't survive the excuses she would come up with to leave him when the real reason was he couldn't do something the average five-year-old could. "I can't even read a bedtime story to Fiona." He looked at her lovely eyes, all filled with pity, and the sight crushed his soul. "I don't know why God made me like this, but He did. I'm dumb, Misty. Always have been, and I always will be."

"No, you're not."

He held up a palm. "Please. I've heard that from so many well-meaning people in my life that I've lost count. 'You have other gifts, Bill. God meant for you to shine, Bill. You're smart in other ways.' "

"People say that because it's true."

"It's not true," he rasped. "I can't read, and I can hardly write more than my own name. I don't even know what the Mother's Day card says that I send to my mom. I just pick out something that has flowers and sparkles." His own bold plans bewildered him. He'd thought he could run a shop? Be a father? The very worst reality came crashing home, obliterating all his idiotic optimism. "I am illiterate. Why did I think I could somehow hide that from a kid I was going to raise?"

Misty's mouth opened, but she did not speak.

"That's why my dad didn't want me to take her in," he said, each word of truth serrated, cutting through his gut as he made the admission. "Dad would have preferred she go into foster care than be raised by her dumb uncle."

"Stop saying that. Fiona doesn't think that."

He shook his head. "But she will. A few months more, maybe a few years down the road, and she'll understand exactly what kind of a dope she's landed with. How's it going to go over when I have to ask her to read her report card to dumb old Bill?"

"Bill," Misty said, stepping close again. "Stop it. Stop saying that about yourself."

I'm just saying it so you don't have to. His heart broke a fraction more as he realized what he had to say next to the woman he loved. "Misty, you're an exceptional lady. I'm sorry. I should have been honest from the beginning. You should not be a party to all of this mess."

"Your learning problem doesn't change how I feel about you."

Oh yes it does, but you're too kind to say so. Her gentle smile tore his heart to pieces. "It's not a learning problem. It's my identity, and it changes everything. I was trying not to admit it, lying to myself really, because I wanted to be with you."

Her eyes glittered with tears. "I want to be with you too, Bill."

Why do I have to be this way, God? Why do I have to lose her? "I can't have a relationship, Misty. I guess I knew it, but I was fooling myself." He saw her flinch, and it made his tattered heart ache even more. "It's going to take all I have just to be a dad. I'm crippled, don't you see? I'm not going to be a partner with someone who has to read my mail and tell me what the medicine bottle says. I can't do that. Not to you. You are too special to be somebody's crutch."

"You're walking away from me?" Her lips trembled, and he wanted more than anything to fold her in his arms. "From us?"

Throat almost too thick to talk, he swallowed hard. "No," he forced out. "I'm setting you free."

He turned around and trudged back through the shop. Gunther dropped his gaze to the counter he was cleaning, though he had undoubtedly heard every word. It would come as no surprise. Gunther guessed at the truth about Bill when he had helped fill out the preschool forms for Fiona, though Bill had trotted out one of his many "I lost my glasses" excuses. Gunther wasn't fooled, never had been, but Misty hadn't known. She'd actually believed he was smart. *Maybe you should have been an actor, Bill.* Shame nearly choked him, and Bill was grateful he did not have to see pity in Gunther's eyes as he passed.

It took a supreme effort, but somehow he headed up the stairs, knowing that each step took him further out of Misty's life.

Sixteen

Misty stood frozen on the threshold. Outside, Jellybean snuffled through the yard, happily oblivious. Inside, Fiona rocked in her chair, looking at the pages of her book. Misty's emotions assailed her—shock, sadness, fear for Bill, but most of all, hurt.

Bill had abruptly severed the tie between them, the beautiful, rare, unexpected love that she had not thought would ever be hers again. He did not care that she was a square peg, but when she'd seen his raw edges, the real anguished places that he strove to keep hidden, it was too much for him.

Maybe she should be angry. She wasn't sure.

Jellybean scampered over and gave her an inquisitive look that was probably meant as a question along the lines of *What are you doing just standing there?*

She didn't know the answer, so she scooped him up and pressed her face to his silky ears.

Gunther still worked behind the counter, quietly laboring on some luscious round balls.

"So what do I do?" she said to him.

Gunther continued rolling. "Hard thing for a man to admit."

"If he cares about me, why doesn't he let me share the burden?"

He blinked at her behind the lenses of his glasses. "Would you?"

Would she? Had she? The woman who hid behind Skype and texts for most of her adult life? The reality of it bit at her. She wasn't brave enough to peel back the layers and expose her own failings. Her talents, her gifts, her ability to bless others with those attributes she'd kept to herself, firmly hidden, along with the painful insecurities. Why, she wondered, did God dispense such weakness along with His gifts?

Because people are connected through their weaknesses, she thought with a start. She hadn't begun to fall in love with Bill because he was slick and successful like Jack, but because he was humble and real and struggling. He'd let his light shine crookedly through the cracks, and it lit up the world around him. But now it was all over.

Two people made by God to shine, to love, to share, yet they were both prisoners in their own way. She shook her head miserably.

"Bill's a good man," Gunther mused, "even prayed for Lunk. What kinda guy does that?" His knobby fingers never lost their candy-rolling rhythm. "Crazy. Helped me look for that dog every single time he took off. Every time."

"Bill needs help."

"Yeah, but he don't want it. Not from a woman he's fixin' to love."

To love? Could she really be so close to that precious connection only to lose it? Jellybean licked her cheek. "So I should just walk away?"

"I ain't an expert on these things," he said with a shrug, "but it seems to me you can't have a future with a guy who doesn't think he has one to offer."

Jellybean wriggled in her arms, repeating the silent question. *What are you doing just standing there?*

Loving a man who did not want a future with her.

Staying in a town that she was not a part of.

Waiting for an actor who left her and Albatross in the lurch without a backward glance.

Fiona looked up from her books and watched Misty. After a moment, Misty forced her legs into motion and went to the girl. "I'm going to go home tomorrow," she said. "And I'll take Jellybean with me because your Uncle Bill is really busy, and he doesn't have time to care for a dog. Do you understand?"

Fiona nodded.

I'll come back to visit. Those were the words she wanted to say, but they stayed inside her mouth. Fiona did not deserve idle promises. Not after losing both her parents. "I will find a violin teacher for you so you can take lessons if you want."

Fiona put her fingers in her mouth and nodded again.

"Will you…" She swallowed hard against the tightening in her throat. "Will you hug your Uncle Bill for me? He loves you very much, and he needs a hug right now because his heart is sad. Can you do that?"

A small nod this time. Misty kissed her on the top of her head, a different pain added on top of the others when she realized how much she would miss Fiona too.

Before the tears could make it out of her eyes, she lurched out the door, Jellybean whining all the way to the car.

By the time she got behind the wheel, she'd decided that the town of Albatross was better seen in her rearview mirror. The next day, after a long rest and a quick packing job, she would leave all the heartache behind and do what she should have done a week before. Lawrence would or would not show up, and Todd Bannington would or would not pull his investment. She had been a fool to think she could influence either one. Maybe, deep down, she'd been using Lawrence as an excuse to stay in Albatross, near Bill.

It didn't matter. Albatross would become part of her past, a note in her journal, a sweet strain of an unfinished melody.

Bill remained on his knees for the better part of a half hour, praying in confused fits and starts, pouring out the anguish in a tangle of entreaties.

Why? Why can't I be the man I want to be? A man who could provide for Fiona and be a partner to Misty? He hadn't realized how desperately he'd come to love Misty until the truth splashed out, burning like acid. In some sort of adolescent fantasy, he had begun to imagine a life shared with her, filled with her laughter, colored by her music, infused with her gentleness. And now he would have to reimagine his life without her.

The floor was hard on his knees, his fingers clenched until they were sore. The praying did not give him clarity or comfort, so he got to his feet.

The thoughts churned around in ruthless circles. *What did you expect, Bill? That you could hide it forever? Or maybe you figured this time you'd learn to read? Finally, from a few practice worksheets and the help of your kid's preschool teacher? What a chump.*

His phone buzzed and he snatched at it, half hoping, half dreading that it might be Misty. He didn't recognize the number, so he tossed the phone aside. He wanted to take off running, sprinting along the beach until he couldn't muster another step. But he was a father, and his kid was waiting downstairs along with a business he'd invested his life in. There would be no running away this time.

"God, help me," he asked one more time before he straightened and forced himself back downstairs.

Fiona caught him at the bottom step, grabbing him around the knees. Unable to speak for the pain and tenderness in his heart, he lifted her up and held her close to him. She grabbed his ears and pressed her forehead to his, saying without words all that she felt in her innocent heart.

Tears sprang into his eyes. *I'm sorry you got me,* his heart whispered. *I'm sorry your parents died, and that I can't be a better father like the one you lost.* He clung to that little child who did not yet realize the truth, dreading the moment that it would all change and embracing each second of the love she offered.

The bell clanged. Jack Golding stepped in. Bill blinked hard and cleared his throat, Fiona still grasping each of his ears. Bill figured he probably looked ridiculous, but there was no way he was going to shake off Fiona for anyone, especially Jack.

"Oh, hey there," Jack said. "This must be your daughter. She's a cutie-pie."

Bill didn't correct him. "Looking for some chocolates?"

Jack smiled. "Just figured I could pick up a gift box or something." His gaze took in the contents of the counter. "Vivian over at the hotel said Misty has been helping out here. I thought I might catch her."

"Too late. She's leaving," Gunther put in.

Bill hid his surprise.

"Leaving the shop?"

"The town," Gunther said. "She's taking Jellybean and going home tomorrow."

Of course she would. Bill had given her no reason to stay, and since there was zero hope of finding Lawrence, she would return to her quiet apartment. He swallowed hard.

Jack smiled. "And here I was hoping she would rethink her dinner plans. Todd wants to stay over until Friday and do a little fishing and see for himself if Lawrence is going to show up."

"Guess you'll have to eat by yourself," Gunther said gruffly.

"Could be." Jack waved a hand. "Pack me up a pound of your best chocolates, my man."

Gunther pulled on a clean pair of vinyl gloves and began loading up a glossy white box.

"Hold on, better make that two pounds." Jack winked at Fiona. "If Misty's not leaving until tomorrow, I still have time."

"Time for what?" Bill asked.

"Time to change her mind about dinner." He paid for the candy and called out a cheerful goodbye as he left the shop with two pounds of Bill's finest chocolates under his arm.

Bill fumed. "Guy like that doesn't deserve a chance with Misty." *Then again*, he thought with a stab of pain, *neither do I.*

On a cloudy Tuesday morning, Misty tossed her duffel into the trunk and carefully secured her violin. She tried one more time to call Lawrence on his cell phone, but as before there was no answer. She saw that she had missed a call from Nana Bett, which she procrastinated about returning. How could she explain to Nana that her cinematic hero had run away like a petulant child and that Misty had been unable to do one thing about it? She thought it best to explain the situation in person as soon as she was safely away from Albatross.

Jellybean stuck his muzzle out the crack of the passenger side window, huffing in snootfuls of air.

"The apartment manager may just rescind his 'pets allowed' policy after a couple of weeks with you." Mr. Jim had a soft spot for animals, but then again, he'd never met Jellybean, the fuzzy wrecking ball.

Though she meant to keep her eyes firmly fixed on the road out of town, they drifted anyway to Chocolate Heaven and the neatly lettered chalkboard sign outside that advertised the Silver Screen Festival. Now she understood that Gunther must have written it all out for Bill. Did it hurt to watch him do it, or was Bill accustomed to being excluded from a world of letters he could not decipher?

Stop it, Misty. Things between you and Bill are over.

Unfinished, like Mozart's incomparable Requiem. But someone had picked up the pieces of that score and finished the work. She hoped someone would come along for Bill, a woman with whom he felt he could fully share his life. It pained Misty that it had not been her.

Those green eyes and that rich laughter. Would she ever drive them from her heart? She'd done it with Jack, hadn't she? But Bill was so very different, embedded deeper in her soul and mind than she'd ever thought possible.

She was about to make the turn toward the highway when out of the corner of her eye a block away she saw Vivian Buckley directing a truck as it backed up into the side lot of the Lady Bird property.

Vivian Buckley.

She'd shared a deep connection with Lawrence, and for all of Vivian's angry protestations, Misty suspected there might be some remnants of affection smoldering deep down.

"You don't suppose…" she said, earning a look from Jellybean. "I mean, if he's trying to reconnect his wires or whatever it is he's about, maybe he might have given Vivian a call."

Jellybean cocked his head and barked twice.

"All right. We'll give it one last, quick effort, but you will not be harassing Tinka, do you understand me?"

The dog barked again. Was that a canine yes or no? Just to be safe, she tied Jellybean's new ultrastrong leash around a sturdy elm that shaded the front of the property, earning herself a derogatory look from the dog, which she ignored. It would take him a good while to chew through that restraint, so she figured a quick stop would be okay.

The Lady Bird's charming backyard was undergoing a face-lift for the festival as two workers unloaded several round tables and white chairs under Vivian's strict supervision. Tinka came over and sniffed lethargically at Misty's shoes.

"What's the matter, Tinka?" Misty asked, giving her a scratch. You seem down in the dumps today."

Vivian walked over and scooped her up, looking around suspiciously.

"Don't worry. I tied Jellybean up."

"Good. I don't need any more dog trouble. Tinka has been moping around for the last few months, right about the time Lawrence showed up."

"What's got her down?"

"I don't know. I think it's her thyroid. She's put on a little weight."

Misty figured if she was anything like Jellybean, she'd been happily helping herself to tidbits from the kitchen, though none of the extra calories ever seemed to stick on Jellybean.

"I'll take her to Doc Benson soon, but I've been putting it off, honestly, because she doesn't like going there. The man could stand a lesson or two in bedside manner." She sniffed.

"Ah." Misty realized she'd run out of small talk and it was time to work her way to the point, but she was unsure exactly how to go about it. "Uh…setting up for the Silver Screen Festival?"

Vivian rolled her eyes. "Yes, though it might be a whole lot of trouble for nothing. There's a storm in the forecast. I have four tables booked for the Silver Screen Tea, and all that money will need to be refunded if you-know-who doesn't show."

"That's why I'm here, actually. I've been having some trouble tracking down Lawrence, and it occurred to me that maybe he might call you."

She goggled at Misty. "Me?"

Misty had obviously thought wrong. So much for keen detective reasoning. "Yes. It was just a thought."

"And just why do you suppose he would do such a thing?"

Misty's face went hot with embarrassment. "Well, um, you two knew each other quite well before he got famous."

"Yes," she said bitterly. "And once he got what he wanted, what he craved more than anything else, he dumped me and never looked back."

"I think maybe he got what he thought he wanted, but he's not so sure anymore."

Vivian's mouth twitched as she thought it over, fingers absently stroking Tinka. "We used to talk about his dreams while we ate bologna sandwiches on the beach. Back then I was always a part of those dreams. 'When I hit the big time, Vee, we're gonna see the world together,' he would say." She sighed. "I never wanted to see the world anyway. I just wanted to make a home, but Lawrence never really knew what a home was in the first place, so I guess that was my big mistake." Misery nestled in her eyes, and Misty knew Vivian's love story was left unfinished too.

"I'm sorry," Misty said.

Vivian's eyes shone with unshed tears. "You know, the funny thing is, I'm the one who loved the real Lawrence. And everyone else, all those adoring fans, they don't even know him." She twirled a lock of Tinka's silky hair. "Love and adoration are different. That's another thing Lawrence never understood."

Maybe he is beginning to, Misty thought. It occurred to Misty then that the true blessing was to know someone, truly know them, and love them, warts and all.

Like Bill knew her? Like she wanted to know him? She fought down a sudden clog in her throat.

"Anyway," Vivian said, hefting Tinka more securely, "I've got a million details to attend to for this ill-fated festival, so if you'll excuse me."

Misty was left alone with the workers, watching them unload for a party she was beginning to seriously doubt would ever happen.

A hand touched her shoulder, and she whirled around.

"Just my luck," Jack said, beaming. "I was getting ready to call you after my breakfast with Todd. I called yesterday too, but you didn't pick up."

She hadn't even heard the call. Her head was too full of clattering emotions after Bill ended things.

The annoying heat suffused her face, which she knew meant she was blushing madly as he stared at her. "Oh. Well. Here I am." *Brilliant repartee, Misty.*

"Yes, here you are, still in town. I want you to have dinner with me."

"I don't think that will work, Jack. I'm on my way back to San Francisco right now."

"But you'll be back, I've heard. I'd make it lunch, but I've got more talks with the movie people."

"Um…"

"Let me ask you, now that we're away from the set. Is Tucker really returning?"

Her heart thudded. "Uh, why would you ask? Is Todd having doubts?"

"Just a feeling I'm getting, though Vivian tells me you know Lawrence pretty well."

"I wouldn't say well exactly…"

"So the truth then. Is Tucker AWOL or what?"

"I, uh…um, what did Vivian say?"

"She said you're going to bring him back on Friday."

"Ah."

"Yeah. She said the town is banking on it."

Banking on it. Banking on her.

"That's the plan. For sure." It wasn't a lie, but it was painted with a coat of shiny optimism she did not feel.

"Since you'll definitely be around on Friday, we can book dinner for then if today doesn't work."

Sucking in a deep breath, she screwed up her courage. "I don't think so, Jack," she said, stepping back a pace.

He sighed. "I understand. I'm not that dense. I know I hurt you when I broke things off. I don't have the right to push my way back into your life, and I'm not trying to, but at least let me buy you dinner and talk. I miss your friendship, Misty."

And the truth was she'd missed his too until she'd met Bill. Jack was handsome, yes, the same charming man she'd been gaga for. He hadn't changed a bit.

But she had. Same square peg in a round-hole world, but lately it didn't seem to bother her quite so much.

"I don't think it's a good idea to have dinner."

He sighed. "Okay. I get it. But if you change your mind, I'll be at the Lady Bird on Friday night since Lawrence is supposed to kick things off with a speech here. Maybe I'll see you after all." He touched her arm and walked away.

A speech? Friday? Cold prickles raced up her arms.

The town is banking on it.

What exactly was she supposed to do about that?

Seventeen

Bill looked at the worksheets until his eyes burned. It started out like it always did, clear and understandable, the way the letter *B* curved around like a fat man with his belt cinched in, Dina told him when she'd run out of more adult language. Then the *A* and the rest of the letters that he learned spelled the word *barn*. He knew it, he understood that those four letters together in that order always said *barn*, but for some reason his eyes had to be convinced every time he saw the words. Or perhaps it was his brain. He wasn't sure why he was practicing anyway.

'Cuz maybe someday, some way, you're gonna learn to read, you big dope. Or possibly that stubborn spark of hope would eventually die. It would be kinder if he would just stop hoping, trying, banging his thick head against an impenetrable wall, but deep down he half believed he'd find that teacher who could crack through his thick cloud of slowness.

But that teacher wouldn't be Dina, and he could not let it be Misty. The thought of her shocked face when she'd understood his illiteracy still made him hot with shame. He read the word three more times, just to be sure, before he put the papers back in their spot on the old, battered desk.

He was relieved that Fiona seemed relatively relaxed for the preschool drop-off. It was like Misty said—she seemed to have let go of the whole winter recital fiasco. He wished he could do the same. Still, he tried to plaster on the friendly guy smile as he kissed Fiona on the top of the head and she walked hesitantly toward the book corner.

"Hey there," Dina said to Bill after she greeted Fiona. "Don't you owe me some paperwork?" The last part came out softly so the other parents wouldn't hear, but there were none nearby anyway. He swallowed.

"No. I appreciate all your help, but I don't think that's going to work out."

Dina gave him a stern look, which he'd seen before in many other instructors. *Do they learn that in teacher college?* he wondered. "Yes, it is going to work out, Bill. I contacted a friend in the Adult Literacy Project, and she's sending me some materials more appropriate than what I've got. It will work if you give it time."

"Thirty-five years isn't enough?" he snapped, instantly regretting his tone. What was he doing sniping at people right and left? "I'm sorry. Please forgive my big mouth. You were kind to try and help. I've gotta go. Lots of prep work to do."

He felt her eyes on his back. *Quitter*, they seemed to say. *You are a disappointment to me.*

Join the gang, he wanted to say.

His father.

His brother.

Fiona.

Misty.

He'd let them all down. Could be it really was time to quit, to finally grow up and face the music. The music did not seem nearly so sweet now that Misty was leaving.

The weight of her departure pressed down on him, slowed his gait until he finally arrived at the grassy expanse that paralleled the main road. This was just the spot, according to the committee, for the Silver Screen family fun area. The field gradually sloped down to a copse of eucalyptus trees and a sandy path that led in twisty fashion toward the ocean. The vision was that folks would tour the movie site, stop in town, spend lots of money, and enjoy the family fun area before taking in the finest beach Albatross had to offer. Presumably, they would then drive home and encourage their friends and family to drop everything and visit the following weekend.

What could possibly go wrong with that plan? he thought morosely as he watched Roger and Toby climbing on the tank they had somehow acquired for the event. It was an impressive sight, perched on the grass, backlit by the buttery winter sunshine like a giant metal insect.

"Hey, Bill," Roger called out. "Can you help unload the boxes from Toby's truck? Need another set of muscles."

Muscles he could do. Waving, he set off toward the top of the hill where Toby's truck was parked, the tailgate down. He heaved a heavy wooden crate out of the back just as a car, Misty's car, pulled to a hard stop next to him. He gaped as she leapt out, clutching her cell phone and closing the door with her hip to prevent a madly barking Jellybean from escaping. He stuck his muzzle out the partially opened window and barked even louder. Misty put a finger in her ear and pressed the phone to her head.

Bill was awash in confusion, embarrassment, and a small measure of elation to see her there. *She didn't come to see you, Woodson.*

"Hold on. Putting you on speaker." She looked wildly at Bill. "It's Lawrence," she mouthed, moving a few paces away from the car as she punched the button.

Bill put down the crate and followed.

She held the phone between them.

"Lawrence, where in the world are you?" Misty said over the barking.

"Is that my Jellybean? I have been in mourning without that little animal. Is he missing me, do you suppose?"

Misty eyed the dog, who was now clawing at the glass.

"Sure, he misses you. Now answer my question, please. Where are you? We've been looking all over."

There was a long silence, punctuated by a chirp. "That isn't important."

"Actually, it is," Misty said. Bill heard the strain in her voice as she tried to stay in control. "You need to come back here. Right now."

A loud sigh from the other end of the phone. "I can't."

"Why not?"

"I'm filled with angst, Misty."

Bill almost smiled at the expression on Misty's face.

"There's plenty of angst going around here too," she said, her mouth tight. "Mr. Wilson is going to shut down the film if you don't return by Friday. Did you know that?"

Lawrence gasped. "So it's come to this."

"As a matter of fact, it has," Misty said. "And there are nice people working on that film, and here in Albatross there are more good people"—Misty flicked a glance at Bill—"who are depending on that movie for their livelihoods."

Bill was grateful that perhaps Misty still counted him as one of the good people. It was something he could hang on to after she departed from his life.

"It is regrettable and tragic but unavoidable," Lawrence was saying. A warbling sound came from the background, like a twittering bird. Nice that the guy was enjoying a park somewhere while Albatross was going bananas in his absence.

"No," Misty said through gritted teeth. "It is not unavoidable. You need to come back right now."

"I am not emotionally centered."

"You're an actor," she spat. "Pretend you're centered."

Bill did not hide his grin this time.

"It's not as easy as all that," Lawrence said. "I am a complicated man, and I find myself mired in regret. The years I've wasted…"

"Look," she said in a gentler tone, "I know you're having a hard time. Parts are difficult to get, and maybe you feel a little bit lonely without…I mean…without a wife or girlfriend."

"Or friends," he said quietly in a tone that had lost its grandness. "I have no friends either, except for Ernest."

"And me," Misty said after a deep breath. "You have me."

A long pause. "Ulterior motives. You're just trying to get me back to the set."

"I'm trying to get you to own up to this situation," she said. "Come back. Meet your commitments. Talk to Vivian. Face the things that seem insurmountable." Again her glance flicked to Bill. Her cheeks reddened, and he felt his stomach tighten.

"Who will help me?" Lawrence said, voice thin and almost childlike.

"I will," she said after a breath.

"Why? Why would you do that?"

"Because that's what friends do."

She looked so strong in that moment, with the wind setting her hair dancing, the light of determination reflected in her chocolate gaze. Bill knew it was not her natural tendency to step out on a limb, into a scary place of uncertainty. He marveled that women were so strong in that quiet, resolute way that was often unseen and unnoticed. Women were the glue that kept families together, and that took more strength than any brute muscle could provide. If Misty had been faced with illiteracy, she would have conquered it. The thought made him look away in shame.

"You didn't choose to be my friend," Lawrence said. "You were hired."

"Well, I'm choosing to be a friend now. When you said God made me to let my light shine, maybe He wanted me to shine it on you."

Silence. Bill's own heart beat thunderously loud in his own ears. *"Face the things that seem insurmountable."* With Misty? Had God meant for her light to shine on his darkest shame? For one brilliant moment, hope lifted up inside him, buoyant and beautiful.

But the burden would be too heavy as the days went by and he saw no progress, no change, no future. She needed a successful man. Someone like Jack. He studied his scuffed boots as the quiet ticked on.

"That is…remarkable," Lawrence said.

"I guess it is," Misty said, a quizzical smile on her lips. "Now please, Lawrence. Come back to Albatross. We need you here."

"Ah, I am very sorry, my new friend, but it is not possible."

She blinked. "Yes, it is. I will come and get you wherever you are. Just give me the address, and Jellybean and I will hit the road right this minute."

"Dear sweet, naive Misty, I am so sorry to disappoint you."

"Then don't," she said. "Where are you?"

"I feel as though it is a million miles away, as if I'm steeped in another world."

"Tell me your location here on planet Earth," she snapped. "Street name, city, latitude, longitude, whatever."

"I must go now."

"Don't you dare hang up, Lawrence Tucker!"

"Goodbye, Misty."

She white-knuckled the phone. "I mean it, Lawrence. I've hiked up and down the coast and interviewed taxi drivers and pried magic wands from your dog's mouth, not to mention the fact that he ate all my pencils and peed on the doormat."

"Misty…"

"I have had enough of playing the detective, chasing you like some nutty terrier. You need to tell me where you are right this minute!"

Misty and Bill heard a sudden series of noises as Jellybean whirled around the front seat in a blur of black. The window buzzed down when a paw or nose found the button on the door panel, and in a flash Jellybean hurtled from the car and leaped for the phone in Misty's hand. The surprise attack knocked the device free and sent it on a spiraling trajectory away from the car.

With a cry, Misty dove after it, looking frantically on the ground several yards away, where the phone had come to land. Bill joined her as they pawed through the tall grass.

His foot kicked the buried phone and sent it tumbling.

"Here, here!" he yelled, scrambling as he finally got the thing.

She clutched at it. "Hello? Lawrence? Hello? Are you there?" Her face went slack as she perused the screen. "It's dead. The screen is crushed. And he didn't even tell me where he is."

They stared at each other, and Bill tried to think of something helpful to say.

He'll call again? Uncertain.

We'll find him somehow? We? He could not be Misty's partner in this escapade, not anymore.

You should just go home and forget about the whole thing.

But the cost of that decision would be disastrous for Albatross and for Chocolate Heaven.

While he rifled through the ideas, he gradually became aware of shouting from the bottom of the slope. They turned in unison to see Misty's VW rolling madly downhill, Jellybean chasing merrily behind.

Misty finally understood the saying "frozen with shock." For a good fifteen seconds, she could only watch in horror as her car began to edge away, tires rotating faster and faster, plowing through the patchy grass. By the time she commanded her feet to start working and run after the escaping vehicle, Bill was already in hot pursuit, legs churning as he sprinted to catch up, hollering out a warning.

Misty added her own. "Look out!" she screamed as the men working on the tank leapt out of the way. The car was heading right for the enormous metal monster.

Her stomach dropped to her feet. It was going to happen right before her eyes. Her car was going to ram straight into the historic tank that someone had gone to great trouble to borrow. Would it damage the tank or shred her car into unrecognizable shrapnel? Both or either would be disastrous. Breath heaving, legs struggling for balance on the uneven ground, she ran as fast as she was able.

She passed Roger, who had dived out of the way, his mouth open so far she could see a wad of blue gum glistening inside.

The front fender narrowly missed a card table, tearing down a poster board sign that read "Buy Tank Tickets Here."

"Sorry!" she yelled to the shocked woman holding a roll of masking tape. Faster and faster the car barreled on, closing the distance.

No, no, no, she thought. *This cannot be happening*. Just when she thought the collision was imminent, Bill caught up with the runaway car and yanked the driver's side door open.

Half in, he cranked the wheel, which caused the car to start on a new trajectory away from the tank.

Yes! she said silently, since she had no more breath left to spare. Now he would be able to get a foot on the brake and stop the thing. Relief flooded her senses, but only for a moment.

Before he got his legs in the front seat, Bill stumbled, and the vehicle outstripped him, gaining speed as the slope steepened.

Bill and Misty and the sprinting Jellybean continued in hot pursuit until all three pulled to a stop, gasping for breath. The car rolled the last few yards and shot out of view down the steep grade.

Three seconds later there was an earsplitting crash.

Lungs burning, calves quivering, Misty forced herself to stagger to the edge and look down. On the grass near her feet was the rearview mirror, which had gotten shorn off and catapulted backward. Her car was wedged sideways between two eucalyptus trees, the rear tires spinning. The only consolation was that the trunk seemed to be relatively intact, so maybe, just maybe, her precious violin had escaped destruction. No, she thought ruefully, that was not the way her life was going at the moment. Her instrument was probably a twisted wreck of spruce wood and steel-core strings. Why not? The car was wrecked, Lawrence was holing up in some mystery location, and she could not seem to escape the town where she did more harm than good.

Bill seemed to sense her thoughts. Without a word, he made his way down to the wreck and reached into the squashed interior, popping the trunk release.

She held her breath while he rummaged around, returning with her beloved instrument and her duffel bag.

"Uh, the violin looks okay," he said. "Much better than the car, anyway."

They stood in silence as the festival helpers came skidding to a stop next to them.

"Wow," Toby said. "You couldn't have got that car stuck between those trees if you tried. Incredible."

Roger whistled, and the card table lady shook her head, still trailing a strip of sticky tape. "You're going to need a special kind of tow truck to uncork that thing. I'll call over to Twin Pines for you and see if they can help."

Revived by the sight of the violin and hopeful for a song, Jellybean sat up and barked.

The shrill noise snapped Misty out of her reverie. "You," she said, glaring at the dog. "You ruined my car."

Jellybean cocked a listening ear.

"You caused me to lose track of Lawrence again."

The dog ran a pink tongue over his nose.

"You don't deserve a song or biscuit or anything else."

Jellybean snaked his tail back and forth in a playful arc, happily indifferent to the chaos he had just created.

"Jellybean Tucker, you are a canine wrecking ball!"

Jellybean rolled on his back and offered his tummy for a scratch.

It was all too much. She cradled the violin case with trembling fingers, resting her head against the hard side. How she wished the earth would suck her up in one mighty gulp, whisking her away from all the people who now stared at her, alternately shaking their heads and marveling at the wreck.

Misty began to sob, her tears dampening her violin case. She could see through her hysteria that Bill was uncertain. After a moment more of hesitation, he closed the distance between them and wrapped his arms around her. It was a gesture she should not have accepted, but she found she did not have the power to move away.

"I'm sorry," he said. "I know I'm not who you want to see right now, but at least I can give you a hug, right?"

No, she wanted to say. *You can give me no such thing, Bill Woodson.* Instead, she put her forehead onto his shirt and sobbed for all she was worth.

Eighteen

Bill stayed with Misty. It seemed the right thing to do in spite of what had happened between them. He could not walk away and leave her there with a crushed car and a terror of a dog. So Bill stayed, embracing her until she was out of tears, and tried to talk through some practical next steps regarding tow trucks and rental cars.

When the tow truck driver arrived, he let out a hearty guffaw and announced they would need a bigger rig, which would not be available until late the following day as it would have to be dispatched from yet another town.

"In my opinion you ought to just leave it there," the driver said. "Could become a tourist attraction. You never know."

Misty did not appear to see the humor. She sat cross-legged in a patch of shade, staring gloomily at her crushed car, her violin case in her lap. Bill wanted desperately to comfort her, but his was not the support she needed. At least he could give her a ride, so he offered to escort her back to Chocolate Heaven and drive her back to her trailer after he stopped to fetch Fiona.

She didn't seem eager about the arrangement, but at least she hadn't outright declined. What's more, she allowed him to collect Jellybean, though the looks she shot at the dog were venomous.

"It's like he wants to destroy me, to keep me prisoner here in Albatross," she muttered.

I should thank Jellybean for that, Bill thought, recalling that it was the naughty dog who brought Misty into his shop in the first place. Painful though it was to consider what he'd lost, he would always be grateful that he'd gotten to know her.

After the preschool pickup, Fiona was thrilled to find Jellybean in the backseat of the van and immediately set to work scratching him in all the places that made his eyes roll in pleasure. Jellybean seemed not the least contrite for the disaster he'd caused. Bill admired his ability to hold on to the positives in life. An idea dawned.

"You know, I was thinking," Bill said.

Misty continued to stare ahead, drumming her fingers on the violin case.

"It seems like Jellybean might not be a good fit for your apartment, and he causes all kinds of trouble in Albatross, so what about Ernest?"

She glanced at him. "Ernest?"

"Yeah. He owned Jelly for a while, and the dog gets along great with Gumdrop and Jujube. Maybe he'd take him back for you."

A smile spread across her face. "You think he would?"

"You could call him and ask," Bill said.

"That's a great idea," she said. "Why didn't I think of it?"

He would have offered a funny remark if things were different, but his good humor was at an all-time low, so he fetched the phone from his glove box and handed it to her.

She glanced at the screen. "You have three missed calls and a message from the same number."

"Yeah?" He was not in the habit of checking his phone because he didn't really understand half the buttons on it, and he'd never figured out how to get to the messages. He kept his eyes on the road. He could not bring himself to ask her to check for him. *Exactly why you let her go, Bill. Don't forget it.*

"I'll check it out later."

Misty called Ernest. When she hung up, her whole body sagged in relief. "He's going to take Jellybean until Lawrence shows up, if he ever shows up."

"Awesome. When?"

"He said anytime, so I could bring him right now, if…" She hesitated. "If you can give me a ride, I mean."

He squirmed. "I, uh, really should be back at the shop." The real truth was, he was reluctant to spend a moment more with Misty than he had to. The shame and the yearning were too great.

She gazed out the window. "I understand. Sorry I asked. It was thoughtless."

"No, I get it. I mean, the dog just totaled your car. Let's go right now. It's okay."

She tried to talk him out of it, but he was determined. If she could off-load the dog, it would be one more step toward getting what she wanted—to leave Albatross for good. *It's the right thing for both of us,* Bill told his churning stomach.

She chewed a fingernail as they drove along until he couldn't stand the quiet. "What's on your mind?"

"Something Jack said. I saw him at the Lady Bird yesterday."

Jack. The name made his jaw muscles clamp down tight. They'd been making dinner plans, he figured. Why not? Jack was a real man, the kind who came with an education and a bright future. With an effort, he kept his tone level.

"What did Jack have to say?"

"That Lawrence was supposed to give some sort of speech Friday night to kick off the Silver Screen Festival. I wished I'd had the chance to tell him on the phone. He might have come back just for the opportunity to address his fans directly."

"Maybe he will call again."

"Then I'd better stop somewhere in Twin Pines and get a new cell phone, just in case."

"Right." They traveled on. Fiona slept with Jellybean curled up on her lap.

"Adorable," Misty said. "You'd never guess in real life Jelly could be such a handful."

"Fiona too. Sleeping, they look like angels."

Bill's phone buzzed.

"Missed call again?" he asked.

"No," she said, looking at the screen. "A text this time."

His mind began to spin. What if the shop was burning down? Or Gunther had an accident?

He felt her looking at him. "Do you want me to tell you what it says?" she said softly.

Because you can't read a simple sentence?

His skin flamed hot.

Let her, he told himself. Let her see the kind of life she was getting away from.

"Yes," he choked out.

"It's from Catherine Anderson."

His head jerked toward her. "Catherine Anderson? That's Fiona's aunt."

"The one who was overseas?"

"Yeah. What does she say?"

Misty read the message. "She said she's been calling and calling. She's on her way to Albatross right now. Actually, she'll be at your shop within the hour." Misty's eyes opened wide. "Better turn around, Bill. I'll get Jellybean to Ernest later. Let's get you back so Fiona can see her aunt."

"She's never shown much interest before."

"Maybe she's come home for a while. Where does she live?"

"Georgia, I think, when she's in the States. Long way to come just for a visit."

She studied his face. "I'm sure that's all it is. Just a surprise visit."

Misty's calm reasoning did not totally erase the nervous twinge in his gut.

Bill drove faster than he should have, and they arrived at Chocolate Heaven within the hour. He lugged a cranky Fiona out of the car. Her hair was sticking up in all directions, and she was not at all pleased to be awakened from her nap. Jellybean wasn't either, but Misty clipped him to his leash.

They entered the shop to find Gunther up to his elbows in yellow rubber gloves and a wide lake of brown chocolate on the floor.

"Conching machine's busted, and I tipped it over trying to fix it. Place is a mess."

Bill groaned, trying to restrain a wriggling Fiona. "Hold on, Fee. I don't want you in the chocolate."

Fiona wriggled harder, turning her body into a floppy fish that Bill struggled to hold on to. "Stop it, Fee."

But she would not stop. Flailing was added to the wiggling, and Bill was not able to hang on. She slid from his arms, and he only barely managed to grab her hand to keep her from falling. Held by Bill's grasp, her feet hit the chocolate and skidded out from under her, splashing both of them in melted goo.

Jellybean raced forward, tugging on the leash and trotting right into the chocolate before Misty could stop him. She hauled him back but not before his torso was sticky, his muzzle dripping from where he'd tried to lap it up.

"Chocolate is poison to dogs," Gunther hollered. "Don't let him eat any more."

Misty snatched him up, and he promptly shook his coat, vigorously splattering her, Bill, the screaming Fiona, and the woman in the white jacket and pants who stepped through the door at that moment.

The lady recoiled as if she'd been struck. "What did I just get all over me?"

"Chocolate," Bill said weakly. "Hello, Catherine."

Jellybean strained to get close enough to the newcomer to welcome her properly, but Misty kept him back.

Catherine dabbed at her jacket with a napkin she pulled from the nearby table. "Hello, Bill." She looked down at Fiona and smiled. "Hey there, sweetie. You're a sticky mess."

Fiona stopped thrashing at last. Jellybean whined, flopping his ears and sending more chocolate flying.

"I'm sorry, Catherine. It's good to see you, but we've had a little chocolate accident," Bill said. "Can you give me some time to get things cleaned up and we can start this visit over?"

A frown creased her brow. "I only have a few minutes before I have to present a report to an overseas client, and that might take a long while. I'll just go check into the Lady Bird, and we'll try this again tomorrow morning, okay?"

He nodded. "Can I...are you just here to visit your niece, by the way? I was just wondering if there's any other reason."

"A visit, yes." Her eyes drifted across the splattered shop. "And to talk about a possible new arrangement. We could have talked on the phone before. I called a half dozen times."

"Sorry about that," Bill said. He did not even try to offer a lame excuse.

Catherine waved a hand. "No harm done. See you tomorrow."

The bells accompanied her departure.

His eyes met Misty's as she held Jellybean, her own clothes doused with chocolate. Bill could not read much of anything, but he deciphered the meaning behind Catherine's words just fine.

A new arrangement.

He saw in Misty's worried gaze that she'd gotten the same message too.

Nineteen

Misty scrubbed Jellybean twice against his forceful protestations, and still he smelled slightly of chocolate. Vanquished and pitiful, he sat on a blanket that Misty had graciously thrown on top of her bed in the trailer. Dinnertime came and went, but she had no appetite for anything. All she could do was pace in unsatisfying circles and wonder what was going on between Bill and Catherine.

Without a cell phone, Misty could do nothing. There would be no chance of connecting with Lawrence again, no opportunity to return Nana Bett's call unless she borrowed a phone from one of the movie people or called from Bill's shop. Though she desperately wanted to know how Bill was feeling about Catherine's surprise arrival, she was afraid to barge in on a tenuous family situation. She was not family, not a girlfriend, not anything to Bill Woodson, she thought with a pang.

After she slipped on pajamas, she passed the hours scrubbing the stains out of her clothes and playing her violin. Jellybean listened with rapt attention as she soothed them both, her music sad and poignant.

As darkness came, the first splatters of rain hit the trailer roof. Of course. There was nothing else that could happen to work against these Albatrossians and their festival. Now the weather was conspiring to ruin the festivities too.

What other factors could possibly conspire against Bill Woodson, already enduring an enormous millstone around his neck? What else? How about if Catherine had arrived with the intention of taking Fiona away? She tried to picture Bill without Fiona.

His life would be so much easier if he were to give up his parenting role. The pressure to hide his illiteracy and to provide for a child would be lifted from his shoulders.

Yet she had a feeling that losing Fiona would also break Bill's heart beyond repair. Carefully putting away her violin, she climbed in bed. Jellybean scooted up tight, snuggling against her tummy.

"Jelly, what is going to happen to Bill?"

The dog curled up tighter, letting out a soft whine as he closed his eyes and went to sleep.

With a deep sigh of her own, she said her prayers and tried to do the same.

⁓

Misty and her canine bedmate overslept until well after ten on Wednesday morning. The movie people were already hard at work, sliding a camera on a long track as they presumably filmed the segments without their star. Misty dressed quickly, fed Jellybean, and looked furtively out the window to make sure no one would spot her escape, particularly Jack. She was not in any mood to fend off his dinner invitations or face more grilling about Lawrence's whereabouts.

She intended to check on the status of her pancaked car, borrow Bill's van, deliver Jellybean to Ernest's loving custody, and buy a cell phone. More importantly, she hoped to hear that Catherine's arrival was not the harbinger of disaster she had imagined it to be. Then after all that? Well, she couldn't very well leave town with her car stuck in a tree, so her timetable was at the mercy of the tow truck.

When the movie people looked particularly engrossed in their work, Misty eased out the door and walked briskly with Jellybean toward town. The sky was still thick with clouds, but the rain held off, which was a mercy since she had no umbrella. Even with the clouds, or perhaps because of them, the ocean air was fresh and crisp. There was no cacophony of traffic noise, no crush of people, no place, really, in which Misty could hide herself as she walked. Her exposure to the world was the tiniest bit thrilling, she thought as she strode along, and frightening too.

Her nerves prickled and danced as she closed in on Chocolate Heaven. She wouldn't pry. Just a quick stop to borrow Bill's van. Tucking Jelly under her arm, she poked her head into the shop. Gunther was wiping down the counter. His face was more lined than usual, a scowl deeply grooving his face.

"Good morning, Gunther. I came to ask Bill if I can use his van."

He jerked his head toward the door. "Outside."

Figuring it would be a waste of breath to attempt any more conversation with him, she let herself out the side door.

"I don't want to embarrass you," Catherine was saying. She was neatly dressed in slacks and a blue silk top with a casual blazer tying it all together. Bill stood across from her, hands on the hips of his white apron. Fiona was on a chair, peering over the back gate to spot a rabbit. Jellybean pulled the leash from Misty's hand and ran to Fiona. Neither Bill nor Catherine seemed to notice.

Misty edged quietly around to retrieve the dog and make her getaway.

"But there are hindrances to you raising Fiona," Catherine was saying.

"Hindrances," he echoed.

"You know. Difficulties."

"Yes, I know what the word means."

"Of course."

"Why don't you say it? Just say it, Catherine."

Misty's heart lurched.

Catherine folded her arms around herself as if she were chilled. "You're making this harder than it needs to be."

"Say it," Bill said. "Tell me why you don't think I can be a good parent to Fiona."

"Purely a practical decision. I can give her a better life," Catherine said calmly. "I've arranged my career so I will be doing less travel. I have financial resources that you don't have, and you..." She sighed. "Bill, you're a good man, and you've done an amazing job with Fiona."

"So why are you the better choice?"

Catherine's voice dropped. "You know why."

"Tell me."

Misty's mouth went dry as Catherine cleared her throat.

No, don't say it, she pleaded silently. *Please don't.*

"Because you're illiterate."

The word fell like a bomb.

Illiterate.

Bill stared at her as if he hadn't heard.

"I wish you hadn't backed me into that corner, Bill. I do not want to demean you in any way. You are a fine man."

"But I'm not..." He cleared his throat. "I'm not smart enough."

"I know you're smart, but let's be realistic. Reading medicine bottles? Understanding school report cards? Planning her financial future? Those are important things."

"Yes," he said slowly. "I know."

"It's not just me. Your father..."

Misty went cold at the look of defeat on Bill's face.

Bill squeezed his eyes shut, and Misty could see the pain that crashed over him in a mighty tide. "I know. My father thinks I'm not fit to parent Fiona."

"He knows…we all know you love her, but sometimes love isn't enough."

Misty felt the thoughts tumbling out of her mouth, leaving her aghast at herself.

"Yes, it is. Bill's a great father."

Catherine cocked her head. "Who are you, if I may ask?"

Bill found his voice. "Misty Agnelli. She's a friend."

"A good enough friend to know that Fiona and Bill love each other very much," Misty continued.

"I am sure of it, but things change, and if we look logically at the situation, it makes perfect sense."

"Bill's her guardian."

Catherine brushed the bangs from her face. "Yes, but in a legal challenge…" She shrugged, and the truth hit home to Misty. Catherine was right. If she brought the matter to court, what judge would rule in favor of a single man who couldn't read? Anguish nearly closed off her throat, and she watched Bill's eyes change as he came to the same conclusion.

He looked at Misty. "Thanks, Misty, I appreciate it, but nothing Catherine has said is untrue." His throat convulsed. "She is the better choice for a parent."

"No, Bill. You are," Misty said from a brave place inside her she hadn't known was there.

He shook his head, eyes glistening. "If she goes with Catherine, she'll get everything she needs. Maybe she'll start talking again soon, and she won't live in a tiny room above a candy shop."

Catherine nodded. "I've already spoken to a wonderful specialist in Georgia about her mutism." She put her hand on Bill's arm. "And you will always be her Uncle Bill. You're welcome to come anytime. I want her to have a close relationship with you."

Misty was paralyzed at what was taking place.

He watched Fiona play, mouth tight. "You'll want to spend some time with her, get to know her better before you"—he cleared his throat—"before you take her."

"Actually, I'd like to fly back home on Friday. With Fiona."

"Friday?" he croaked. "So soon?"

"I think it would be best to make the transition quickly, don't you? Easiest on Fiona?"

Bill didn't answer.

"Is it okay if I spend some time with her now?" Catherine asked.

"She has to go to preschool," Bill said after a moment. "She has school from one to four today. It's important for her to be in school every day, Miss Dina says. She's smart," he said desperately. "She knows all her letters, and she can write her name with a capital letter in the right spot."

"All right. How about I pick her up from preschool, and we can play at the beach for a while? I'll bring her back to the shop about six?"

"But…but maybe we should both be there. She might be scared without me."

Catherine held up a hand. "Bill, let's do what's easiest for Fiona, okay? A couple of hours to reacquaint ourselves is going to help things along immensely. It's not as though I'm a complete stranger, you know. She and her parents stayed at my house last time I was in town. I was at her christening and her last birthday party."

"I…I guess you're right," Bill said.

No, no, no, Misty's heart cried.

Catherine called out, "Fiona, can you come here a minute, honey?"

Fiona approached, a smear of dirt on her forehead. Catherine knelt next to her. "Do you remember me, Fiona? I'm Auntie Catherine, your mommy's sister. You've stayed at my house before."

Fiona did not respond except to stick her two middle fingers in her mouth.

"Remember my dogs, Buster and Charlotte? They loved playing with you in my swimming pool. I'd like you to come back to my house with me and stay with me and the dogs, okay?"

Fiona blinked, unresponsive.

"Tell you what. Today after your preschool is over, I'll pick you up and we'll go get ice cream and play on the beach for a while. How would that be? You like ice cream, I remember. Vanilla, right?"

Fiona nodded.

Misty looked on in absolute disbelief. This couldn't be happening. Not to a good man like Bill.

But Catherine was nodding, walking back out of the shop, and Bill was standing silent, watching her go.

"Oh, Bill," Misty said when the door closed. "I'm so sorry."

He was quiet for a long moment. She ached to comfort him.

"Will you…" He cleared his throat. "Misty, will you help me with something?"

"Of course. Anything."

He led the way back into the house and up the stairs to the battered desk in his bare room. A new set of workbook pages lay there, the top one with handwritten words to practice.

He took out a red construction paper heart with a picture glued crookedly in the middle. It was a shot of Fiona perched on Bill's shoulders, holding firmly on to his ears. They were both grinning.

"We're making Valentines for the kids for next month, but Dina knows I usually need a lot more time to get mine ready, so she gave it to me early. I want to give it to Fiona before…" He fisted his hands on his hips and exhaled. "Before she leaves."

Misty found her throat was too constricted to answer.

He grabbed a purple marker from a cup on his desk. "Could you write something for me?"

Misty nodded, sitting down on the chair and uncapping the pen.

"Write…'Uncle Bill will always love you.'"

Through a blur of tears, she wrote.

Bill walked Fiona to school, each step feeling miles long. He sought out Dina and delivered the news.

"Her aunt?" Dina said.

He nodded. "Fiona is going to live with her."

Dina's mouth widened in an *O* of surprise. While she struggled to hide it, he bent to kiss Fiona. "I'll see you back at the shop when Auntie Catherine brings you home, okay?"

By the time he'd straightened, Dina had herself under control, handing him an envelope, which he knew contained the next few words he'd asked her to help him master. Though there hardly seemed to be a point anymore, he took the papers and exited quickly.

On the front step, he found himself immobile. He knew he should be hard at work preparing chocolates just in case some people arrived for the ill-fated festival, but he didn't have the heart to go back there. The prospect of a long afternoon stretched before him, and he realized how he'd learned to schedule his day around Fiona. The preschool drop-off. Dinner preparation and bedtime ritual. They were the duties that defined and gave purpose to his hours. How precious it all seemed now that it was evaporating before his eyes.

"Bill."

He blinked and discovered he was now standing on a corner, Misty idling next to him in a dented Subaru with Jellybean scrabbling at the rear window.

"Isn't that Gunther's car?"

She nodded. "He loaned it to me. I didn't want to bother you about the van. I'm going to take Jellybean back to Ernest. Do you…I mean…would you like to come along?"

"I'm not real good company right now."

"That's okay. You know I'm no good at small talk anyway."

For some reason, Misty's words brought a smile to his face. He climbed in, and Jellybean immediately launched himself from the backseat to the front and gave Bill a thorough tongue swabbing.

"Man, this dog can't decide who his owner is."

"I think that's the problem. He refuses to be owned. That way he can love everyone the way he wants when he wants."

Bill sighed. "Must be nice."

Misty drove along, and they lapsed into an extended quiet. Soon she would be gone too, he thought. No Fiona to give his life purpose. No Misty to wrap his heart in joy. The scenery passed in a blur until they arrived in Twin Pines.

Misty bought a cell phone and immediately checked her missed calls.

"Two from Nana and none from Lawrence."

The whole hide-and-seek game with Lawrence seemed suddenly ridiculous to Bill. How small, how frivolous it was in the face of what he was losing. "Misty, did you really think you could save this whole Silver Screen Festival by bringing him back?"

"No, not at first."

"What made you change your mind?"

She considered. "You did."

"Me?"

She didn't look at him. "You saw something in me that I didn't."

He stared at her in amazement.

Pink blooms appeared on her cheeks. "That 'shine your light' thing. You made me want to do that."

And how he lived for that light, yearned for it, and grieved the loss of Fiona, of his pride, of Misty. "I'm glad," he said sincerely. "I am very glad."

"And I wish I could do that for you."

There's nothing left inside me to shine, he wanted to say. His brain did not work right, and now, in the time it took for Catherine to blow into town, his heart was beyond repair as well.

He opened his mouth and then closed it. *Please don't say anything else, Misty. Not another word.* He could not take it.

Instead, she held out her hand and took his, the fingers squeezing, soothing, just being there, sharing space. Jellybean added his own fuzzy comfort, stretching out on Bill's lap and laying his bony wedge of a head against Bill's knee. Bill closed his eyes and settled back against the seat, allowing the bump and squeak of the old car seat to soothe him.

∽

The car ground to a halt, and he opened his eyes. It was two o'clock, and he automatically thought about Fiona. It was snack time, so she would be enjoying goldfish crackers and apple slices.

You're going to have to stop measuring your life in Fiona time.

They piled out and knocked on Ernest's door. No answer to the knocking or their calls.

"What's this?" Bill said. He picked up a note that was tucked under the doormat.

"Sorry," he read as he handed it to Misty. Sorry. Five letters, and he'd read them. A bitter victory. Sorry was right. Too little, too late.

"It says he had to go take his sister in Redding to the hospital because she broke her wrist. He is staying overnight, and he won't be back until tomorrow."

Bill looked at Jelly, who turned in a tight circle in an attempt to catch his tail.

"Looks like you're foiled again, Misty," he said.

Misty braced her hands on her hips and stared at Jellybean. "You're harder to get rid of than a case of poison oak."

Jellybean rolled over for a tummy scratch.

"Oh, okay," Misty said, reaching for the wriggly belly. "But you're going to have to get used to someone else giving you these scratches pretty soon."

Unperturbed, Jellybean closed his eyes to enjoy the moment.

Oh, to be a dog, Bill thought. No regrets, no unmet potential. No cares about the loneliness of tomorrow. He sighed. It was time to return to Albatross and begin the countdown to Fiona's departure.

∽

When they arrived back at the shop, Gunther immediately untied his apron. "Neighbor said Lunk's busted out again. Gotta go find him," he grumbled as he made for the door.

The clang of the bells faded away. Bill stood in the empty store while Misty tied Jellybean to the lamppost. The silence was palpable. No more kid noise, the squeak of her rocking chair, the barnyard boogie music from her CD player. Just quiet.

He tried to rouse himself. He had work to do, floors to clean, recipes to prep, yet still he stood there, steeped in the silence, paralyzed by it.

Misty came close.

"Are you okay?"

He forced a nod. "Just realizing how different it will be when Fiona is gone."

Her face shone with sudden passion. "Why don't you fight for her, Bill? You can be her parent. I know you can."

He let out a long, slow breath. "Isn't that what being a parent truly is? Wanting the best for your child? Catherine can give her a better life than I can."

Even if he could finally tackle his illiteracy. Catherine had money, a home, his father's blessing—everything a child could need.

"But she thinks of this as her home, of you as her father figure."

"She'll…" He cleared his throat. "She'll forget that in time. She'll forget about me."

Misty bit her lip between her teeth. Then she wrapped him in a hug, stroking his back and pressing kisses on his neck.

His heart thrummed a tune, and he marveled at how the world went away when he held her, the softness of her cheek erasing the bitterness, the brush of her hair stirring some warmth back into his soul, and he allowed himself to accept the comfort.

"Bill," she said, looking up at him, lips trembling. "I love you."

Time stopped ticking. He jerked, staring now at the red-blushed face looking up at his. She'd said it. He hadn't been dreaming.

This woman who could not face a roomful of people without breaking into a sweat had just bared her soul and lit a fire in his. *"I love you."*

He put his hands on her shoulders and lost himself in her brown eyes. She loved him enough to see the man he was, not the man he couldn't be. Could Misty Agnelli really be meant for him?

Then the doubts rushed in, pushing back the joy and assailing him with practiced ease. He wanted to say, "I love you too," but the words stuck fast, just like they always had, his snare, his ruin.

"Misty, I can't believe how blessed I've been that you stumbled through the door of my shop."

She smoothed the front of his shirt, smiling shyly. "Me too."

"But…" The brown eyes looked suddenly uneasy, and he hated himself for what he had to do. "I won't let you confuse pity with love."

"I'm not confusing it," she said.

He put a finger underneath her chin and tilted her face up to meet his gaze. "Look at me." His other hand traced the smooth perfection of her cheek. "Look in my eyes and tell me you don't feel sorry for me."

"I don't," she breathed, but he saw the flicker there, the small waver of doubt that told him the truth. It hurt so much he almost couldn't stand it. There was pity mixed in that love. *Poor Bill.* He would not make her say it aloud.

"Misty, I will never forget you."

He felt her stiffen, forced himself to let her step out of his hold. She fled for the door.

"I'm sorry," he said as the door banged behind her.

Twenty

Misty lay in bed, watching the clock tick away the hours until five thirty a.m. Her mind replayed her incredulous admission to Bill.

"Bill, I love you." Her mouth had actually allowed the truth to gush forth. What was happening to her, and why in the world had she let it slip out?

She loved him. And yes, while an element of pity was mixed in because he had just lost his daughter, her love was much more than that. But Bill would never believe it, and never again would she make a fool of herself in such a spectacular fashion.

And that's what happened when you stepped out, spoke up, and bared your soul. *Way to humiliate yourself, Misty.* The combination of Bill's rejection and her own mortification made her want to hide under the bed again. She might possibly have tried it, except that Jellybean would have thought it a game, and she'd never get him calmed down again.

As it was, he was hopping out of bed, nosing aside the trailer curtain in search of the first signs of dawn. There weren't many,

187

only raindrops chasing each other down the glass and a cloudy, gray sky. From far away came the chirp of some stalwart bird that wasn't intimidated by the storm. *Nutty bird, don't you know your nest is the safest place to be?* The twittering continued.

A bolt of inspiration sizzled through her. Chirp. Bird. The sound in the background noise during her phone call with Lawrence. She sat up so fast her head spun.

It could not be.

She had to be mistaken.

Five thirty a.m was far too early to make the call, but she made it anyway, receiving no answer.

Jellybean was whining now, eager to go out in spite of the storm.

"Oh, we're going out, all right," she snapped, tossing the covers aside. "We're going to get Lawrence and haul him back to Albatross whether he's done with his crisis or not."

She was flinging on clothes and charging for the door. Jelly turned in excited circles as they plunged into the rain and headed for Gunther's house.

He answered the door clad in flannel pajamas with one eye open. "What are ya doin' here so early?"

She explained, leaving out the part about why she was not about to ask Bill to use his vehicle, and he shoved the keys at her, probably just to get her off his doorstep. They were on the road, zipping through the rain and arriving at Nana's Berkeley apartment in just over forty-five minutes. Misty pounded on the door in spite of the early hour. Inside she could hear Nana's canary, Peepers, chirping away, as he had been during her phone conversation with Lawrence.

Nana opened up. "Well, here's the girl who never answers her phone. Do you know how many times I tried to call?"

"There'll be no small talk." Misty held back the jumping Jellybean, fixing Nana with a hard stare. "You're harboring Lawrence here, aren't you?"

Nana blushed. "Well, I would not actually use the word *harboring*. He was having a sort of crisis, you see, so I've been praying for him, and my friends have been too. I think we're making inroads."

"Your friends?"

"Yes, we've worked out a visitation schedule." Nana winked. "They all want to see him, of course, so we keep strictly to the time limits. A big star like that, right here in our complex?" Nana shook her head. "But I made them all promise not to Tweet or put it on Facebook since Mr. Tucker is here in secrecy. And no Snapchatting—definitely none of that. Everyone loves him, and he's been passing out boxes of chocolates, which didn't hurt either."

"Why didn't you leave me a message?" Misty wailed.

"I was actually going to get a taxi today and come and tell you in person. Mr. Lawrence said phones can be tapped. I didn't want to take any chances. We've almost got him convinced he should go back."

Misty resisted an eye roll, hauling Jellybean to the kitchen behind Nana, where she found Lawrence sipping coffee and munching on a bagel.

His eyes lit up when he saw Misty and the dog.

"Jellybean, my angel!" The dog leapt and pranced in joyful circles around Lawrence's chair. "Well, look at that. He really did miss me," Lawrence said, reaching to scoop Jellybean up.

The dog skirted just out of his reach.

"You can bond in the car," Misty said. "I'm taking you back to Albatross."

"But I'm not ready," he started. "I'm feeling—"

"Listen," Misty said, cutting him off. "You can have all the feelings you want later. Right now, you're going to go back to save the day."

"I am?"

"This is your moment, Lawrence. You have confused reality with your acting world for too long, but now is the time to be a

real-life hero in your own story, not a made-up plot or a script."
She swept an arm in a grand gesture. "You have a chance to save
a whole town."

Lawrence suspended the coffee cup in midair. "I do?"

"Yes, so you're going back." Misty would have played an inspi-
rational theme on her violin if she'd had it handy. "For Albatross
and for Vivian."

"Vivian?" He grimaced. "I'm not sure I can do it."

"Yes, you can. And Jelly and I are going to help you. We'll write
your speech on the way."

"Speech? What speech?"

"You're kicking off the Silver Screen Festival tomorrow with a
riveting talk."

"I'm not feeling at all riveting," Lawrence said, brows drawn. "I
think I should stay here and let Bett take care of me for a while longer. She's very good at bolstering the soul."

Misty grabbed him by the elbow, eliciting an encouraging bark
from Jellybean. "No more bolstering. Come on, Mr. Tucker. Time
to let it shine."

The rain slowed to a patter by Thursday noon. Bill took Fiona
to preschool along with some chocolate treats for the class, since
the next day would be her last before the move to Georgia. He
ignored the lurch in his stomach. Again, Catherine would be picking Fiona up from school and working on bonding with her. Bill
had packed Fiona's suitcase. How was she feeling about the move?
Bill had no idea.

His feelings had seized up like ruined chocolate, and even working with his beloved peanut butter crunch filling did not revive
him. What was there to do but move on to the next recipe and the
next, to fill up Chocolate Heaven with as many sweets as he could

to ease the bitter pain of losing Fiona? Vivian roared into the shop just as he was finishing dipping the handmade marshmallows.

Her eyes were wild, and her normally neat hair hung loose about her face. "She's gone. I can't find her anywhere."

He was about to ask who until his brain kicked in. "Tinka?"

"She ran out of the yard early this morning when I went out to dry the tables."

He was already hanging up his apron. "I'll help you."

"Thank you," she said, mouth twitching. "Um, I heard that Fiona's aunt is here to take her to Georgia."

Bad news did indeed travel fast. "Yes."

"For what it's worth, I think you would have been a great father."

He looked away. It was the second time someone had expressed confidence in his parenting. He felt an odd nudge in his gut. *Maybe... No, it doesn't matter, Bill. Sometimes love isn't enough, remember?* Hoping circumstances would miraculously change was grasping at straws, and he could not allow it. Catherine was right. "Thank you."

Though they scoured the town for a good hour, there was no sign of the spoiled dog. Vivian returned, despondent, to the Lady Bird, and Bill went back to his duties. He was surprised to see Gunther's car speeding toward the film set. What in the world could the old man want there?

Stifling his curiosity, he tried to while away the hours until six o'clock, when Fiona would return. Catherine had promised more ice cream and beach time if the weather cooperated. He hoped Fiona wouldn't get a stomachache from all the treats.

Another thing he would have to train himself to stop worrying about.

Toby and Roger came into the shop in search of a snack just before closing time.

"All set at the family fun area. Tank's all shined up and ready. Never did get Misty's car out, but we'll just add it in for ambience."

Toby popped a fresh chocolate-dipped marshmallow into his mouth. "There's some doings over on the set."

"Yeah?" Bill said. "Like what?"

"Dunno what it's about, but there's an awful lot of barking."

He wondered if Tinka had snuck over. Leaving the shop in Gunther's hands, he pocketed his cell phone and trudged up the gravel path. As he approached, he heard Jellybean's high-pitched bark and saw Larry sprint across the lot and up the steps into his trailer.

Larry slammed the door and hollered out the window. "Get that monster away from me."

Misty ran into view and grabbed the trailing leash. Panting, she yelled, "Sorry, Larry. I lost track of him for a minute."

Bill's heart jumped at the sight of her. She spotted him and ducked her chin.

"Hey," he said, pasting on a smile he did not feel. "I thought maybe I could find Tinka here. Have you seen her?"

She opened her mouth to answer when Lawrence rounded the corner, his face tinted with stage makeup, garbed in a soiled infantry uniform.

Bill gaped. "Mr. Tucker? Where did you come from?"

"He was holed up at Nana's house," Misty said. "She was providing soul bolstering and home cooking. She couldn't leave me a message because she was afraid the phone might be bugged."

Bill stared from Misty to Lawrence. All he could do was laugh. This would happen to no other lady, in no other town, in no other corner of the universe.

"So I guess the festival is on then?" Bill said when he'd stifled his laughter.

"I guess that's what it means, all right," she said.

"Did you say, my good man, that Vivian is missing her Tinka?"

"Yes, as far as I know."

The phone in Bill's pocket rang. He answered.

Catherine's panic-stricken voice was audible even to the others. Bill listened, horror flashing through him. In the time it took for Catherine to get the words out, the bottom fell out of his world again.

"I'll be right there," he said, then he ended the call.

"Bill, what is it?"

"Fiona's lost."

Misty did not skip a beat. "We'll take Gunther's car. I'll drive us back."

"Come on," she said to Lawrence. "You can come and help look since your shooting is done for the day."

"But…" Lawrence started.

Misty didn't give him time to answer. She just hauled him by one arm and Jellybean by the leash. If he wasn't so worried, Bill would have stopped to admire the way she had taken charge of the addled star and his dog.

As it was, he raced to the passenger seat and willed the vehicle to move faster as they sped back to Albatross.

Catherine met them at the door of Chocolate Heaven with the *Barnyard Boogie* book clutched in her hand. "We came back here to get her a pair of dry shoes. I took a phone call, and when I was done, she was gone. We were going to read a story."

Bill bolted up the stairs to check the bedrooms, returning in moments, face tight with fear. "Not there."

"The back door is unlocked. She could have let herself out," Misty said.

"I've looked in the yard already," Catherine wailed.

They piled out anyway. There was no sign of which way the child might have headed imprinted on the rain-soaked grass.

Bill checked the gate that led to the empty field. "It's not fully closed, so she might have gone this way." He yanked it open and charged out, shouting Fiona's name.

The only reply was the breeze blowing across the tall grass.

"Fiona!" they yelled, fanning out and looking in all directions.

"The beach," Catherine said. "You don't think she might have gone there herself, do you?"

Misty considered the roiling surf, and her skin went cold with terror.

Catherine dropped the book and set off at a run toward the sand. Lawrence picked it up as if it might be a clue to Fiona's whereabouts.

It suddenly occurred to Misty that they had among them a searcher with better skills than any of them. She unclipped Jellybean. "Where's Fiona, Jelly? Can you find her?"

He bounded off immediately, cutting a path in the wet grass, his bark carrying through the wet air.

Misty tried her best to keep up, stopping breathless about fifty yards away, where Jellybean parked himself, barking at something she could not see. Bill and Lawrence pulled up next to her.

"Where?" Bill said.

Misty dropped to her knees. Almost overgrown with grass was a wooden cover, the rotted middle broken out. Misty pushed away some bits of wood and used her phone's flashlight to peer through the gap. It was barely sufficient to pierce the gloom, but Misty knew without a doubt what lay at the bottom.

"Here!" she yelled. "Fiona's fallen into some sort of drainage pipe."

Bill crouched down and stuck his head in the pipe. "Fiona!" he shouted. "Are you in there?"

Far away from down in the darkness came the sound of a child crying.

Twenty-One

The opening to the drainpipe was wide enough to allow Bill to attempt to shove his torso in, with Misty and Lawrence holding on to his legs to anchor him.

"I can't reach her," he said, as they dragged him out. "I'm going to have to get a rope. Gunther's got some. I'll be back as quick as I can." He gripped Misty's arms. "Stay with her?"

"Yes. We'll call 911 and keep her calm."

He squeezed her shoulders, and she kissed him. "We're going to get her out."

She saw his Adam's apple move as he swallowed convulsively, and tension radiated through his touch into her.

Another moment and then he raced away.

Misty leaned over the hole. "Fiona, we're up here. Uncle Bill has gone to get a rope to pull you out. We'll stay with you till he gets back, okay?"

Jellybean was barking hysterically, and Misty could hear Fiona wriggling.

"Stay still, honey." She wasn't sure how deep the drainage pipe went, but if the child slipped any farther, they might not have enough rope to reach her. They had to do something to calm her down. What tools did they have? She was a musician without a violin, and Lawrence a man lost so deep in pretense he had to run away from the real world.

Her gaze wandered to Lawrence, who appeared completely befuddled, gripping the storybook and shifting his weight from foot to foot. Maybe, she thought, just maybe it was time to let Lawrence do the thing that God made him to do.

"Lawrence," she commanded, pointing to the *Barnyard Boogie* book he held. "You have to act it out for her."

"Huh?" he said blankly.

"The book," she said. "It's Fiona's favorite. Read it with all your acting tricks and make it come to life."

"But…"

"We have to keep her still so she doesn't fall farther down."

He looked from her to the book and back again. "I'm not really a hero, Misty. I'm a fake. I pretend."

"Then pretend for all you're worth, Lawrence."

"I'm no good at real life." The gloom made him appear so much older, the dim light catching each crease and wrinkle.

"You're going to be great now, Lawrence."

"How do you know?"

"Because there's a little girl's safety at stake, and somewhere down inside you there's a real-life hero." She put a hand on his shoulder. "Please."

Lawrence stared at her. Jellybean barked and pawed at Lawrence's shin. He looked down at the dog as if he'd never seen him before.

Misty nodded in encouragement. "Go on."

"Do you really believe I can help?"

"Yes, Lawrence, I do."

Slowly he lay belly down on the wet grass, holding the book over the edge of the hole.

"Fiona, it's Mr. Tucker," he said softly.

"Louder, Lawrence."

He gave her another tentative look and then sucked in a deep breath.

"Fiona, stay still," he boomed in a voice that echoed and made Jellybean stop in his tracks. "And listen to the tale unfold."

Misty thought for a moment that she had made a mistake. Maybe Fiona would be even more scared at this strange turn of events, but Lawrence continued, voice loud and reverberating as if he were performing *Hamlet* at the Globe Theater. "The barnyard was full of fun," he began, "the day the cow came to play." And then he launched into a performance complete with various accents, including a Southern drawl for the cow and even snatches of song in his surprisingly pleasing tenor.

"'Hooray!' said the horses, munching their hay," he intoned.

Jellybean sat enthralled, and Misty would have as well if she had not been so worried about Fiona. She peered into the hole, and she could just catch the white gleam of Fiona's upturned face as she listened to her favorite story being told by the world-famous star of stage and screen.

Misty's vision blurred as she watched him read, emotions rolling across his face like the storm clouds as he put everything he had into the performance.

He'd reached the last page, and Misty was about to tell him to read it again when Bill sprinted up, rope in hand, Catherine trailing behind along with a panting Gunther.

Gunther tied one end of the rope around his own skinny waist, and Catherine, Misty, and Lawrence grabbed hold too, bracing themselves as Bill looped the other end around his own middle.

"I'm coming down to get you!" Bill shouted. "Hold on, Fee."

He let himself down into the hole headfirst as the others strained against the taut rope.

The fibers cut into Misty's fingers as she held on for dear life.

"We're slipping," Catherine gasped.

They leaned back, their feet digging into the wet ground, struggling to anchor their shoes in the soaked grass. Gunther was nearly lying flat on his back, his skinny arms tensed with the effort. Time ticked on as they strained to hold their position.

"Pull us up!" came Bill's muffled shout.

"He's got her," Gunther gasped. "Heave-ho on three. One, two…"

They yanked against the weight, but the rope didn't seem to move.

"Again, on three," Gunther grunted, and once more they hauled. This time the rope began to yield. Slowly, inch by painful inch, they pulled.

When it seemed to Misty that her trembling muscles could not hold out any longer, Bill was pulled clear of the hole. His face was turned away from her, his hair tangled with dried leaves.

Misty blinked against the drizzle that had begun to fall, not daring to let go of the rope. She did not see Fiona. Her pulse jackhammered. Had he not been able to reach her? Had he lost hold of her during the ascent?

In the distance came the faint sound of sirens. Would the emergency responders be too late?

Finally, she saw why Bill did not straighten and get to his feet immediately. He had both hands locked around Fiona's wrists as he slowly pulled her from the drain.

When they were clear, Gunther dropped the rope, and Lawrence and the women did the same. Fiona was cuddled in Bill's arms, sobbing aloud while he sat cross-legged, rocking her.

"It's okay, baby," he crooned. "Uncle Bill's got you."

His hair was standing up, dirt caking his cheek and a dribble of blood snaking from a scratch on his chin. But nothing could hide his relief or the desperate love he felt for Fiona.

Catherine knelt next to them, crying, one hand stretched out to touch Fiona's head, yet stopping short of the contact.

"I'm so sorry," she said. "She could have…"

The thought was better left unsaid, Misty figured.

Jellybean yipped and licked every part of Fiona he could reach. When he was done, he circled back and pawed Lawrence's knee. The medics arrived, parking on the road near the shop and then hurrying across the uneven ground. Bill stayed by Fiona's side as they evaluated her while she was strapped onto a gurney. Misty scooped up Jellybean, and she and Lawrence edged back to stay out of the way. Bill left with the medics, insisting that he accompany Fiona in the ambulance.

"Lawrence," Misty said, kissing him on the cheek. "You were magnificent with that story."

He smiled a shy, innocent smile so unlike the smug Hollywood grin. "I guess I was, wasn't I?"

"Yes, you were."

He laughed. "I must call Bett and tell her all about it."

Misty joined in the laughter. "Absolutely," she said.

She gathered Jellybean, and they returned to the shop before piling into Catherine's rental car to follow the ambulance with Bill and Fiona back to the hospital.

Catherine drove, her expression stricken.

"I didn't know what to do, but he did," she whispered.

"Yes," Misty agreed. "He's a good dad, and he loves her."

"It's not just about love…"

Misty hefted Jellybean. "Yes," she said without hesitation. "Yes, it is."

Bill was relieved beyond belief that Fiona had not suffered any serious injuries. Catherine, Lawrence, and Misty waited the long hours with him at the emergency room after securing Jellybean at Chocolate Heaven. Catherine deciphered the forms and insurance information. He should have been mortified that he could not deal with the paperwork himself, but he could feel nothing but profoundly thankful to God. It was a new sensation to not bother hiding his illiteracy.

After Fiona had been properly checked out, Misty gave Bill a tentative kiss on the cheek and called a taxi to return to Albatross and escort Lawrence and Jellybean home to their trailer.

Bill and Catherine finally arrived back at Chocolate Heaven with their sleepy charge. He carried Fiona to her bed and lay down on the floor, letting her twirl his hair to her heart's content. He said a prayer out loud, thanking God for keeping her safe, his child, his precious angel.

Her little fingers kept up their hair twirling. "Amen," she said softly.

He could not hold back tears, though it was his turn to be stricken mute. In his silence, he thanked God again, for the one precious word that promised she would recover and rediscover her voice someday.

After Fiona was soundly asleep, he returned to the kitchen and fixed Catherine a cup of tea.

"I am so sorry," she said for the millionth time. "I should not have taken my eyes off her."

"It's okay. You made a mistake, but you won't do it again. It's part of the parenting learning curve. Trust me, I've made plenty of wrong choices since I started taking care of her. You just learn, one mistake at a time."

"Bill," Catherine said, "I think maybe I've made another mistake too. A big one."

He raised an eyebrow.

She nodded. "When we found her in the bottom of that drain, I was paralyzed, but you weren't. You knew exactly what to do."

He shrugged. "I just reacted, that's all."

She traced a finger along the rim of her mug. "What I saw out there in the field was not an uncle helping his niece. It was a father taking care of his daughter."

His heart beat hard in his chest. "I know I can't be what Dillon was in a lot of ways, but I love her like a father. That much is certain."

"Yes." Catherine wiped at her eyes. "And it would be wrong for me to take Fiona away from you."

Bill stood, hands clasped around his own mug, unable to comprehend what he was hearing.

"Are you saying…"

"That you are the one who should raise Fiona. I will help however I can, and I will be on call twenty-four-seven for anything you need read or deciphered or…or for anything, really, but you are her father."

"I—" he choked out. "I will try every day to be the best father I can be."

"I know." She gave him a tremulous smile. "I'm sorry I put you through all this."

He could not help himself. He put down his mug, picked her up, and whirled her around. She laughed and hugged him until he deposited her back onto terra firma.

"I'd better go. You have a big festival here tomorrow, and I have a flight to catch." She paused at the door. "You know, for a guy who can't read, you taught me a lesson today, and I'll never forget it."

He watched her go, and his heart was so full he didn't think he could get a sufficient breath. The single light burnished the little shop in a soft golden glow, and he was pretty sure his soul was lit up with exactly that same tint.

He sank to his knees, hands clasped. "Thank You, Lord," he whispered. "How can I ever be worthy of such love and blessings?" His eyes traveled to Fiona's sodden book, lying on the counter where Lawrence had left it.

A smile spread slowly across his face as he understood, finally understood, what a colossal fool he had almost been.

Friday dawned with a partially clouded sky and a note from Lawrence tacked to Misty's trailer door.

"Will be there for speech at nine. Must run an errand first."

An errand? He'd taken Jellybean and the leash. She sat up, groggy, checking the time. It was eight thirty. In a state of panic, she dressed, grabbed Lawrence's speech, and jogged toward town, worrying as she went. It was not possible that Lawrence had made a break for it again, was it?

She made it to the Lady Bird in a record ten minutes, hoping to find that Lawrence had finished his mysterious errand and shown up for the kickoff. A crowd of some forty people were seated on white folding chairs in front of a podium set up on a makeshift dais in the front yard. Silver cloth draped the podium, and a large picture of Lawrence adorned the front.

More people were filing off a tour bus and standing behind the erected chairs. Misty's skin prickled at the nape of her neck. She scanned the crowd, catching sight of her grandmother and several of her pals in the front row. Nana waved to her. There was no sign of Lawrence. Her cell phone told her it was ten after nine.

Vivian approached, dressed in black, her eyes shadowy with fatigue.

"Well? Where is he?"

"I don't know. He had to run an errand, he said."

"If he doesn't show in another five minutes, people will start to leave," she hissed.

"He'll be here," she assured Vivian. *I hope.*

Clutching the speech in her hands, she caught sight of Bill in the back row, Fiona in his arms. He looked altogether younger, a wide smile on his face as he jutted his chin at her. Had Catherine booked a later flight so Fiona could experience the festival? His green eyes stood out in the crowd—so green, she knew, they would live in her memory long after she'd left Albatross.

Four minutes, then five. A trickle of sweat began to bead on her brow. Where was Lawrence? Had he run away for more centering? Bolstering?

Jack caught her attention with an airy wave as he lounged against the side wall of the inn. Somewhere in the crowd, Todd Bannington probably sat, waiting to see if his investment was a sound one.

Five more minutes rolled by.

Vivian took her by the elbow. "We have to stall. You have his speech. You're going to have to say it."

"Me? Oh no. There's no way I'm getting up in front of all these people."

"You have to."

"What about you?"

"You're his assistant on this film. You have credibility."

Misty's body began to shake. "I don't give speeches."

"It's time to start."

"I can't. I just can't."

Vivian grunted. "Fine. I'm done with this whole thing. I'm going to lie down and wait for all these people to leave once Lawrence disappoints them." She began to make her way through the ever-growing throng.

Misty looked at her shoes, pressing as far away from the crowd as she could. The conversations were getting louder now, the sound crashing in on all sides as the clock ticked away the minutes.

Lord... Misty wanted to pray that God would immediately throw the side door of the Lady Bird wide open to disgorge Lawrence for his anxious fans. Failing that, perhaps a fire alarm or an earthquake to jolt the people away, somewhere, anywhere but their current location only a measly few feet from her. But the rest of the prayer did not come out. Misty's eyes locked on Bill's. He gave her another smile, and she recalled how it felt to let her light shine just a bit through the cracks. To step out of herself to try to bless the town that had twined its way around her heart and the people who had done the same. Was there just a little left to sparkle? One more ounce of light, of courage, to shine out of Misty Agnelli?

Knees trembling, she climbed onto the dais and faced the microphone. The crowd went still, a phenomenon more terrifying than their chatter. Every eye was laser-locked on her, blazing down on her hiding spot under the bed.

Lord, help me, she finished silently before she gripped the microphone in a sweaty fist.

"G-Good morning, ladies and gentlemen," she squeaked. "I am…uh, Lawrence Tucker's violin tutor." She saw Nana Bett elbow the man next to her, face wreathed in an enormous grin. "I…um, since Lawrence is delayed, I thought I c-c-could read you part of his speech before he arrives."

She thought she heard a groan from the throng. Her breath was coming in desperate pants. *I'm going to faint. Right here, in front of all these people and Nana. In front of Bill and Jack and movie lovers from far and wide.*

Sparks danced in front of her vision, and she was almost ready to bolt when she caught Bill's gaze again, so calm and encouraging.

You're doing great, she could imagine him saying. He gave her a thumbs-up.

The paper had gone limp and crinkled in her death grip. She smoothed it out. "So let me start by telling you a f-few interesting things you may not have known about Lawrence Tucker." She'd made it to number three when she realized she could no longer decipher Lawrence's handwriting.

Where was that fire alarm? The friendly earthquake? She tried to swallow, but her throat had gone completely dry. "When will he be here?" an elderly lady called from the second row.

"Uh…well, I am not completely…"

And then, as if cued by the maestro, Lawrence appeared, strolling jauntily past the crowd. Jellybean shot up to the platform, leaping into Misty's arms with such velocity she almost dropped him. Lawrence swept up to the foot of the dais with Tinka under his arm and a loaded canvas bag hanging from his shoulder.

Thank You, God, breathed Misty.

"Tinka!" Vivian shouted, running to take the dog from Lawrence. "You found her," she said, with a look of astonishment for Lawrence. "How?"

"Well," he boomed grandly. Then he paused, sighed, and continued in a voice that was not at all like a stage icon, but very much like a regular man who wanted to help a woman he cared a good deal about. "I heard she was missing, Viv, and I know how much she means to you. Jelly and I have been out all night searching for her."

Vivian blinked very hard and pressed her lips together. She seemed to notice the bag at the same time Misty did. The fabric writhed and undulated.

"What is in that bag, Lawrence?"

With the legendary swagger back in his voice, he said, "You'll never guess, ladies and gentlemen. So let me tell you a story you won't believe."

Twenty-Two

Bill stood with Fiona still on his shoulders to watch Lawrence spin his tale. The man had a gift for gab—that was undeniable. When the audience was about half crazy with wondering, he reached into the bag and began handing the tiny, wriggling things to an astonished Misty. Three puppies in total, the roly-poly creatures eliciting oohs and aahs from the crowd.

Vivian's mouth dropped open. "Tinka? Those are Tinka's puppies?" Her eyes narrowed into slits. "And we have Jellybean to thank for these mongrels?" Her question was lost in the rush of the crowd as Lawrence stepped off the platform to greet his fans personally, wisely keeping one of the adorable pups in his possession. The only thing more irresistible than a celebrity, Bill thought, was a celebrity with a newborn puppy.

Bill went quickly to Misty. "I have to go to the shop," he said. "You were fantastic." He planted a kiss on her cheek. "Come see me later, okay? I need to tell you something."

She nodded. "I guess I'd better go reunite these babies with their mommy. But aren't they funny looking?"

He agreed. The torsos were broad and sturdy, the legs and heads small, giving the dogs an altogether awkward construction. Something about their build was familiar, but seeing the people streaming outside toward his shop, he didn't have time to mull it over. He was knee-deep in customers for the first time ever, and he wasn't going to waste a moment of it.

"Come on, Fee," he said, lifting her into his arms. "Are you ready to go sell some chocolates?"

"Uh-huh." She clasped his ears. He thought she looked particularly adorable today in the yellow overalls he'd picked out with nearly matching yellow bows for her hair. One more reason for people to stop into Chocolate Heaven. She'd have a few minutes to enjoy the festivities, and then Miss Dina had agreed to watch her for the day.

Not one minute after they entered the shop, the bells clanged, the door opened, and in came the flood he had been praying for.

It wasn't until after five o'clock that they were able to close up the shop when the crowds finally thinned. He would be up all night refilling the candy supply, but it didn't matter. They'd done a good day's sales, and there was promise for the next day too and the upcoming weekends. It wasn't a miracle cure for his economic woes, but it would be enough to buy a new conching machine and help pay the insurance that was coming due. After Gunther untied his apron, he retrieved Lunk from the backyard just as Misty entered the shop, followed by Lawrence and Vivian. Tinka nestled in Vivian's arms, Lawrence carried two puppies, and Misty had the smallest one. Jellybean trotted along at the edge of the gaggle, sniffing at the puppies and eyeing Lunk warily.

"You're going to keep these pups," Vivian was saying, "since it was your ill-behaved dog who fathered them. Don't think you can escape your responsibility."

"It wasn't Jellybean," Lawrence said, and though his tone was haughty, Bill thought he caught a glimmer of mischief in the man's eyes. "But Jelly and I will endeavor to help you with your brood. I intend to stay in Albatross after the shoot is over. Retire here, even. It's close to my friend Ernest, and I like the scenery," he said, smiling at Vivian.

She gasped, her cheeks pinking. In an instant, Bill thought she morphed into a high school teen. "Oh. Okay." Then she started in again. "But don't think your dirty dog is going to come around and father any more litters."

"As I said, it wasn't Jellybean. I am a responsible pet owner. He's been fixed. They are no progeny of his."

Gunther walked with Lunk through the door. The dog perked up, droopy body energized as he waddled over to Tinka.

Gunther cocked his head. "More energy than he's shown in…" His words trailed off as the realization that was also dawning in the collected group began to materialize. "You don't suppose…" Gunther started, and then he clapped a hand to his forehead. "Lunk!" he hollered. "*That's* why you were busting out all the time?"

"What? What?" Vivian said.

Lawrence's smile got even broader. "It seems, Vivian, my love, that Jellybean is proven innocent in fathering those pups."

Her horrified gaze traveled down to the lump of a dog at her feet. "Lunk?"

Lunk slurped a wide pink tongue across his fleshy lips. Bill was sure he saw a look of pride on the mutt's face.

Gunther groaned. Vivian slammed out of the shop, Lawrence following with laughter bubbling out of his mouth. Bill and Misty looked at each other, bursting into loud guffaws.

"I did not see that one coming," Bill said.

"Me neither. For once, it wasn't Jellybean who turned out to be the naughty one."

After Gunther lugged Lunk to his car and carted the errant

father home, Bill walked Misty into the backyard, where they watched Fiona searching for rabbits as the sun ebbed low in the sky.

"I was really proud of you up there, giving that speech this morning."

Misty groaned. "It was terrifying. The scariest thing I've ever done."

"I know. That's why it was magnificent. You were terrified, talking in front of a big group like that, and you did it anyway. That's courage if I ever saw it."

She shrugged, biting her lip and looking down. He didn't blame her for being hesitant to talk to him, considering how he'd forced her away before. He'd put the distance between them, and she was doing her best to preserve it.

Fiona approached and tugged on Bill's pant leg.

"Snack time?" he asked.

She nodded. Hoisting her up over his shoulder elicited a giggle as they returned to the shop and Bill sliced an apple for Fiona.

The silence lingered until it was broken by the sound of claws scratching against the front door.

Jellybean looked in quizzically, barked, and then shook his ears before taking off again. Ten seconds later, Lawrence jogged by in hot pursuit.

Bill laughed. "So much for giving up his naughty reputation."

Misty agreed. After they fell into another too-long silence, she asked, "Do you need some help making more chocolates?"

"Are you offering assistance? I thought you were going to hightail it out of town after you delivered Lawrence."

She nodded. "Yes, but I could help for an hour or two. I think they almost have my car uncorked, and Lawrence is back for Jellybean, so I guess everything is in order."

"Almost." His pulse accelerated.

"What's left?"

He picked up Fiona's storybook from the table where he'd left it that morning, and suddenly his nerves turned to ice.

"I…I wanted to tell you that Catherine has decided to let me raise Fiona."

Misty's whole face lit up with the intensity of a shooting star. She threw her arms around him, sending his heart beating even faster. He hugged her close, allowing his joy to mingle with hers.

"What made her change her decision? Never mind. It doesn't matter. I'm so, so happy for you." She squeezed his shoulders, and he held her to him until she pulled away, tucking her hair behind her ears.

"Really. I'm just thrilled for you, Bill."

And he could see that she was. He read the love and kindness warming her face, clear and true, like a torch shining in the darkest of nights. "Thank you. I wanted to say thank you for all you've done, for who you've been to me and Fiona. We…I haven't been good to you, not in the way you deserve. I am sorry for that."

She let him go, looking away. "No need to apologize. You're welcome for whatever I've done. Anyway, I should be going if you don't need help with the chocolates."

"Wait. I want to say one more thing." His palms grew sweaty and his mouth went dry at precisely the same moment. Battling down a sense of panic, he opened the book to the second page and put his finger under the first word. "This part is Fiona's favorite."

Her eyebrows were crimped in puzzlement.

What are you doing, Bill? You're about to make an idiot of yourself.

He cleared his throat. "Barnyard Cow," he started. "Is her… here to stay. W-Won't you come and…" He struggled, feeling that same desire to quit. She was thinking he was foolish, dumb, an illiterate oaf stumbling through a kid's book. But if God could make him a father, He could certainly give him courage enough for this. Swallowing hard, he pressed his finger to the page and forced himself back across the landscape of letters he'd been practicing for days. "Won't you come and p-play today?"

He finished. Two pages. Twelve words. A mere step for most,

a journey for Bill Woodson. He continued to stare at the pages, afraid of what he would see in her lovely brown eyes. Finally, he looked up from the warped book.

She was smiling, tears pooling. "Bill, you did it," she whispered. "You were reading."

"Just a few lines," he said, feeling a surge of pride so strong it nearly choked him. "I can only do the first and second pages, but I'm getting better." He reached up and wiped the tear that had trickled down her cheek. "I'm going to do it, to keep going, because I want to be a good father and a good partner."

"To whom?"

He held his breath. "You."

The light caught her glow of surprise. "Me?"

He nodded.

"But...but you said..."

"A lot of dumb stuff," he finished, grasping her by the shoulders, allowing his fingers to travel up to brush the soft skin of her neck. "I was embarrassed, humiliated...all the things that come from wounded pride that prevented me from seeing what God put squarely in front of my clueless face."

She gaped. "But...me?"

"You. I love you, and I want us to be together forever."

"But I'm awkward and..."

"And patient and shy and courageous and loving and faithful. And you are the square peg I want in my life and Fiona's, if you'll have us."

Her mouth was a round *O* of surprise. He adored her, the curve of her cheek, the earnest gleam of a faithful woman struggling just as he did but with so much more grace for all her clumsiness. And she couldn't see it, not at all.

"I love you, Misty," he breathed, fingers trailing through her hair.

"But you're..."

"Stubborn and prideful and the worst reader on the planet. And I probably don't deserve a woman like you, but I'm gonna greedily grab you for my own if you will accept me because God made us both to shine, and I can't do that if you're not in my life."

"Bill," she said, holding up a palm, "you need to stop talking."

He did, closing his mouth and readying himself for whatever she had to tell him.

"Bill Woodson," she said after a slow exhalation. "I love you and Fiona, but there are complications."

"Like what?"

"Well, I thought I might give a try at giving some violin lessons, you know, in person."

He beamed. "We'll find you a spot here in Albatross or wherever. Ernest will be thrilled."

She was not smiling, which scared him most of all.

"The real problem is…there's another guy."

His stomach fell. A guy. Jack. Of course. Jack wanted her back.

"Oh," he said, puzzled when he caught a glimpse of the sparkle in her eyes.

"He's kinda hairy, funny looking, and probably just as destructive as his adopted Uncle Jellybean, who cannot get enough of him."

"What?" He blinked. "Misty, you're killing me here."

She laughed. "I told Vivian I would take one of the pups."

Bill felt his world expanding, bursting with a light and love that blazed through his heart. "I'm a dog guy. You know I am."

She pretended not to hear. "I think I'm going to name him Truffles, and we're a package deal, so if you want me, you get Truffles."

He pulled her close and kissed her. "Oh yes, ma'am. I'll take Misty with a side of Truffles."

"I love you, Bill."

"I love you too, Misty."

She melted into his arms and they kissed again, listening to the music of the ocean and the faraway barking of a naughty terrier.

About the Author

Dana Mentink lives in California, where the weather is golden and the cheese is divine. Dana is a two-time American Christian Fiction Writers Book of the Year winner for romantic suspense and a Holt Medallion winner. Her suspense novel *Betrayal in the Badlands* earned a *Romantic Times* Reviewer's Choice Award.

Besides writing, Dana busies herself teaching third grade. Mostly, she loves to be home with her husband, two daughters, a hyperactive mutt, a chubby box turtle, and a feisty parakeet.

Visit her on the web at www.danamentink.com.

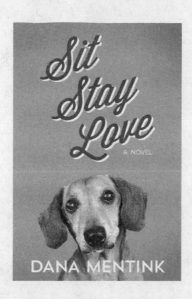

"I've asked everyone from the shortstop to the hot dog vendors, and no one wants a thirteen-year-old mutt."

Pro baseball pitcher Cal Crawford is not a dog guy. When he inherits his deceased mother's elderly dog, Tippy, he's quick to call on a pet-sitting service.

Gina isn't thrilled to be a dog sitter when her aspirations lie in the classroom. Furthermore, she can't abide the unfriendly Cal, a man with all the charm of a wet towel. But with no other prospects and a deep love for all things canine, she takes the job caring for Tippy.

As Gina travels through Cal's world with Tippy in tow, she begins to see Cal in a different light. Gina longs to show Cal the God-given blessings in his life that have nothing to do with baseball or fame. This pro athlete, along with an out-of-work teacher and an overweight, geriatric dog, is about to get a lesson in love...Tippy-style.

The author is committed to donating a portion of the proceeds toward senior dog rescue.

Fetching
Sweetness

A NOVEL

DANA MENTINK

Standing Between Stephanie and Her Dream Is One Hundred Pounds of Lovable Trouble

It should have been so simple for Stephanie Pink: Meet up with Agnes Wharton in a small town in California, retrieve the reclusive author's valuable new manuscript, and be promoted to a full-fledged literary agent.

But Agnes's canine companion, Sweetness, decides to make a break for it before Stephanie can claim her prize. Until Agnes has Sweetness safely back at home in Eagle Cliff, Washington, Stephanie will never set eyes on the manuscript she needs to make her dreams come true.

When Stephanie tracks the runaway mutt to a campground, she meets Rhett Hastings—a man also on the run from a different life and a costly mistake. Rhett agrees to help Stephanie search for the missing dog... thus launching a surprising string of adventures and misadventures.

Once Sweetness gets added to the mix, it's a recipe for love and loss, merriment and mayhem, fun and faith in the backwoods of the Pacific Northwest.

To learn more about Harvest House books and
to read sample chapters, visit our website:

www.harvesthousepublishers.com

HARVEST HOUSE PUBLISHERS
EUGENE, OREGON